Praise for

No One Left to Come Looking for You

"Addictive and fun . . . One original and unpretentious and funny sentence after another. . . . Very smart and very funny, a slangy, brainy, expletive-laden, occasionally touching pleasure to read from the first page to the last."

—Adelle Waldman, *The New York Times Book Review*

"Lipsyte's experiment in hard-boiled hardcore manages to take its self-imposed conventions somewhere more playful and less pointlessly nostalgic than have similar genre exercises by his contemporaries. . . . More dramatically than even Thomas Pynchon, who had to invent a vertically integrated crime syndicate with *Inherent Vice*'s Golden Fang, Lipsyte has updated the detective novel for the billionaire era."

—Lisa Borst, *Bookforum*

"That rare thing: a satiric crime novel that doesn't forsake story for style. It is tightly plotted and pleasingly twisty . . . To reveal the satisfying resolution would be a crime in itself."

—Marc Weingarten, *Los Angeles Times*

"A flaming truckload of humor, wit, and joy . . . A badass book with brains, wit, moral decay, and radical outrage to spare."

—*Kirkus Reviews* (starred review)

"A darkly funny punk noir . . . Lipsyte's eye for detail and ear for dialogue keep the story rolling at a fabulously funny clip."

—Cat Auer, *The AV Club*

ALSO BY SAM LIPSYTE

NO ONE LEFT TO COME LOOKING FOR YOU

A NOVEL

SAM LIPSYTE

Simon & Schuster Paperbacks

NEW YORK   LONDON   TORONTO
SYDNEY   NEW DELHI

Simon & Schuster Paperbacks
An Imprint of Simon & Schuster, Inc.
1230 Avenue of the Americas
New York, NY 10020

First Simon & Schuster trade paperback edition December 2023

SIMON & SCHUSTER PAPERBACKS and colophon are
registered trademarks of Simon & Schuster, Inc.

For information about special discounts for bulk purchases,
please contact Simon & Schuster Special Sales at 1-866-506-1949
or business@simonandschuster.com.

The Simon & Schuster Speakers Bureau can bring authors to your
live event. For more information or to book an event, contact
the Simon & Schuster Speakers Bureau at 1-866-248-3049
or visit our website at www.simonspeakers.com.

Manufactured in the United States of America

1   3   5   7   9   10   8   6   4   2

Library of Congress Cataloging-in-Publication Data is available.

ISBN 978-1-5011-4612-1
ISBN 978-1-5011-4613-8 (pbk)
ISBN 978-1-5011-4614-5 (ebook)

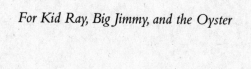

For Kid Ray, Big Jimmy, and the Oyster

No one left here anymore
Everyone's moved off to one side
Decide if you're gonna hide
There's no one left to come looking for you

—Come, "Off to One Side"

He thought of the friends of his youth; they had all been the
friends of his youth, whether he knew them personally or only
by name, whether they were the same age as he or older, all
the rebels who wanted to bring new things and new people
into the world, whether here or scattered over all the places he
had ever known.

—Robert Musil, *The Man*
Without Qualities

The people really are what make New York City great.

—David Dinkins, former mayor
of New York City

ONE

The day after I decide I'm Jack Shit, the Banished Earl steals my Fender Jazz Bass.

Dyl Becker at King Snake Guitars wakes me with a phone call before I even know it's gone.

"Jonathan," he says.

"I'm Jack now."

I stir sugar into a cold mug of yesterday's Bustelo, stare out my smeared kitchen window at the brick facade across the air shaft.

"Jonathan," Dyl says. "The Earl was just in here with your bass. I could tell it was yours from that little Annihilation of the Soft Left sticker on the headstock. Hey, I thought you weren't friends with those guys anymore."

"I'm not," I say, "but it's a pain to scrape that thing off. Did you buy the bass from him?"

"He didn't have the papers. Even if I hadn't known it was yours, I wouldn't have bought it. You've got to have the papers."

"He left with it?"

"Yeah."

"Fuck."

"What's wrong?"

"He'll just trade it for a measly bag of dope."

"Hey, it might not be measly. But yeah, that sucks."

1

While I hold the phone to my ear, I scan the Rock Rook for any other missing objects. Seems like all the other stuff—not much, admittedly, besides some milk crates full of records and books, ashtrays full of the Earl's ash, empty forty bottles, a few chipped dishes—is still here. I've shared this one bedroom on Avenue B with the Banished Earl for about nine months, though it wasn't always a one bedroom. It used to be a studio. We threw up a high wedge of plywood to make a little sarcophagus for the Earl. I sleep on a foam mat near the door.

"Hey, Jonathan?"

"I told you, I'm Jack now."

"As in Jack Shit?"

"Exactly," I say.

"What made you change it?"

"I just like how it sounds."

"Cool."

"Okay. Later, Dyl."

"Wait."

"What."

"I heard you guys are looking for a new drummer."

"Preferably a girl drummer," I say.

"I can be a girl drummer."

"No, Dyl. You don't hit hard enough."

"I hit hard."

"Not in time."

"I'm better, Jona— I mean, Jack. I've been practicing all month."

"No."

It's touching how much Dyl dreams of joining the band, but some were meant to lead, others to follow, and still others to hang around, devoted mascots.

"Well, how about a second guitar player?" Dyl says. "Think about it. A fucking sonic curtain, right? And, no offense, but I've got better chops than you or Cutwolf."

"That's true," I say. "But the very fact you said *chops* disqualifies you."

"What does that mean?"

"Think about it. No offense. I've got to find the Earl."

In our world, you may not say *chops* or *axe* or *jam*. You may say gwee-*tar*, *fish*, *tubs*, *bitch out*, *beat bag*, *bag fever*.

Every subgroup has its own linguistic code.

We're not even a subgroup. We're just the Shits, a fast-disintegrating band. We used to have solidarity. We used to have esprit de corps. We used to have, according to *Sour Mash* magazine, a "scabrous, intermittently witty, post-skronk propulsion not unlike early Anal Gnosis."

But then bag fever set in.

The Banished Earl is the worst. The abscess in his arm is a black, ragged wormhole. You could swan dive into it, time travel, get shot out into the future, the year 2000 perhaps, or a few hundred years in the past. Picture old France. Picture beauty-marked men who prowl and preen, in tights, in wigs. Their skinny swords serrate the air. It's sort of like some of the bars we play. It's sort of like us some nights. The Shits do like to dress up. The Shits are a writhing, shimmering society of the spectacle. The Shits are fierce and noisy and wounded and sad.

The Shits fear not art.

But you may not say *art*.

But you may certainly say that the new year, at least so far, slurps the sandpapery, drippy johnson of a clapped-out rhino.

I'm happy to say it along with you, or even compose a melody, if you think there's a song there, though such retrograde, faux-transgressive vulgarity is not quite our style, even if we are called the Shits. Point is, it's only January and I'm almost broke. My girlfriend, Vesna, has ditched me for good and, perhaps most catastrophically, my J-Bass is gone. Point is, I must locate the Banished Earl before he surrenders my fish for a measly, probably half-beat bag of Tango & Cash, which, if word in the bars can be trusted, is the most undiluted dope east of Ludlow Street. Point is, I need my bass and we need the Earl. If the Shits are not utterly atomized, we have a show at Artaud's Garage a week from this Saturday.

We are guaranteed 13 percent of the door. If twenty-five people come at five bucks a pop that's . . . well, you do the theorem.

I don my thermals and various sweaters and shirts—my mother taught me the laws of layering early in life—and step out into the frozen bleakscape. My city is a tundra. The wind whips in off the river like the river is one of those cool dominatrix chicks just doing it to finance her comp lit degree and the wind is, for instance, a whip. Cutwolf's sister Drusilla was a domme for a time, until she dropped out of the pain game to become a serious cake maker. That's not even a euphemism. She's on the American Fondant Team, flies to Antwerp for major competitions.

I've never been to Europe. I've never been out of the country, unless you count Canada, which I don't. But a dude in Barcelona has been playing our second seven-inch, "Shits for Real," on his indie radio show. He sent us a very complimentary postcard. That could lead to something. A few dates in the Gothic Quarter? A European tour? A person can dream. But not without his instrument. No bass, no band. I hold down the bottom.

I also write the songs. I am not exactly music, but I do write the songs. Or at least the tunes to a lot of them, along with Cutwolf and Hera.

The Banished Earl is our front man, our lyricist and lead screamer. His brief includes but is not restricted to howls, whimpers, banshee shrieks, declamations, provocations, semi-ironic rooster struts, blind dives into the mosh pit, simulated or else revocable genital self-mutilation, and, of course, spectacle. Spectacle above all else.

Though now that the Banished Earl is the Vanished Earl, all bets are off until I find him.

But first, sustenance. The pizza joint on Avenue A boasts a permanent special: two slices and a soda for a dollar fifty. Most days, that's a decent portion of my life savings.

Now I stand at one of the tall, circular Formica tables, shake out some oregano on my oven-blistered slabs. New York pizza is the best pizza, so let's not have that conversation, but I'm not one of those process fascists when it comes to your eating technique. Fold the fucker, eat it flat, cut it into baby bites with a plastic knife, run it through a blender on frappé at home and chug. It's a free country, at least when it comes to stuff that doesn't matter.

Apropos of which, there's a TV mounted over the counter, and right now it shows a bunch of people in overcoats, a formal procession, almost like a funeral if everybody seemed semi-secretly delighted, which I guess is sometimes the case. There is a grinning man with good political hair, a woman in a red plaid coat. Soon the man has his palm on a leather book.

"They all have to drink a pint of pig's blood before they're sworn in," says a gaunt fellow beside me. He's somewhere between twenty-three and seventy-eight years of age, wears a denim jacket over a torn mesh half-shirt and ragged designer jeans that feature these weird smears and stink like he's pissed them. It's a tight look. He plucks a jar of hot pepper flakes off the table, sprinkles some into his mouth.

"Hey!" the counterman yells. "You gotta buy something to use that."

The fellow shrugs.

"Pig's blood?" I say.

"Secret ritual. They all do it. Except Jimmy Carter. He refused."

This neighborhood does crank out the cranks. It's one of our cultural products, like pocket quarterbacks in western Pennsylvania. But who am I to judge? I'm just a relative newcomer, a callow youth with a degree in modern media, a couple of part-time jobs, and a dream of moderate underground success about to swirl down the crapper. Maybe the Denim Ghoul here knows of what he speaks. Maybe this Bill Clinton guy did knock back a nice warm glass of porcine plasma before he strode out to take his place in history.

The Ghoul taps out more spice flakes onto his tongue.

"This fucker," he says, flicks his chin at the screen. "He's from Arkansas. He'll find brand-new ways to ream us. Be like nineteen eighty-four all over again."

"The book or the year?" I say.

The Ghoul nods.

The funny thing is, I read *1984* *in* 1984. Perhaps this makes my perspective unique. I cried when Winston's mother gave him the lion's share of the rationed chocolate, kept none for herself and just a sliver for his sister. I realized what an un-grateful prick I'd been to my mother and would have been to my sister, if I'd had one. It was a depressing year, what with the cruelty and tedium of high school in New Jersey and my father running off with a paralegal from his office. I missed him, but I didn't miss the fights, my mother in tears every night, though in a way it was worse after he left, my mother's fury on full blast, me the stand-in for millennia of dickwaddery.

"When you grow up," she said, "just promise me you won't be one of those men."

"Which men?" I asked.

"Any of them. All of them."

My father returned to the farce after six months to reprise the role he'd originated, and they live together in occasionally tender detente to this day, but in the interim I spent a lot of hours brooding in my room. I'd stare at the water stain on the ceiling made by our leaky roof, write bad poems about staring at a water stain, beat off. It wasn't the most nuanced adolescent experience.

But one day I discovered music. Not the kind on the radio. I knew all about that. Some of it, the older stuff, the records my mother played when she did her calisthenics, I adored. But the newest FM pablum made me gag, this music designed by robots for consumer zombies. It was death by a thousand saccharine-sweet cuts.

This older guy, a neighbor, decided to join some snake-and-drum cult in Florida, had to divest himself of worldly posses-sions. He gave me a ripped A&P shopping bag full of punk rock records. I brought them home and put them on my turntable, each one a revelation, an orgasmic punch, a shock like I'd licked a terminal on the world's tallest battery. Ferocious and exquisite sound realms beckoned. I'd found the answer to my anger, my suffering. I got monastic, studious, bought a cheap bass guitar, a Hondo. Four thick, glinting, nickel-wound strings: What could go wrong? I wrote a song called "Stain of Water." The rest is not yet my place in history.

TWO

"Jonathan."

"It's Jack now."

"Since when?"

"Since yesterday."

The Earl's ex, Hera Bernberger, stands in the doorway of her apartment on Third Street, near the Bowery. She's not only the Earl's ex, she's our ex too. Ex-drummer. Yes, the departures were related. The sloppiness of the Earl's drug habit drove her away from him, and the sloppiness of our chord changes drove her away from us. Now she plays in a self-regarding minimalist duo with a dildo named Wallach. He's a conservatory graduate, one of those smug skill-bullies, a music reader.

I follow Hera into her apartment. I haven't been inside it in a while, but it looks the same as when the Shits used to muster here, the warm lamplight filtered through amber and magenta shades, the imitation leopard-skin pillows on the divan, the glass bones she blew years ago at art camp on the walls, the throne-like chairs, carved from teak, shipped up from her late grand-mother's house in Key Biscayne. We each now perch on one of these great, wooden seats. Hera lights a menthol cigarette, takes a ponderous drag, the kind that asks, *Shall I now train my powerful and pitiless intellect on the problem of you?*

"So, why Jack?"

9

"Why what?"

"Why Jack?"

"I don't know. Why Hera?"

"Because my stupid hippie mother named me that."

"Is Hera hippie?"

"It's not Moonbeam. But it's pretentious, educated hippie, sure. So answer me: Why Jack?"

"Because . . . like . . . Jack Shit."

"Okay."

"You get it?"

"I get it. But Jack Shit is a cliché."

"That's why it's interesting."

"Because it's stupid?"

"I'm deconstructing it."

"Are you?"

"I think so."

"But I always thought Jonathan Shit had a certain elegance. Plus, your name is actually Jonathan."

"I won't be a victim of happenstance."

"And I won't be a victim of you just showing up whenever and annoying me. I'm not sitting around with my thumb up my bum. I'm embarked on an aesthetic journey here."

Hera stands, brushes ash from her maroon coveralls, her standard winter uniform. She waves toward the room, I suppose to indicate evidence of her artistic embarkation, but all I see is a drum pad, a few disconnected patch cables, an empty jug of chardonnay, some scattered take-out menus. You can always tell when her anger is genuine. She doesn't bust out borrowed idioms like "bum." Hera hails from the Gold Coast of Connecticut.

"Sorry," I say.

"What is it you want?"

"Your boyfriend stole my bass."

"You know I'm not with Alan anymore."

Alan is the Earl's given name.

"Has he come around?"

"He was here last night. He was all fucked up. Left some clogged works in my bathroom. Really disgusting. I wish he'd go back to snorting. He's in bad shape."

"What did he want?"

"First he said he wanted to get back together," Hera says. "I told him no way. Then he just wanted money."

"You give him any?"

"What, are you a detective now? The Case of the Missing Bass?"

"Stolen bass. You give him any money?"

"Twenty bucks. All I had on me."

"Big mistake," I say. "He can't handle that much cash."

"I just wanted him out of here."

"Did he say where he was going?"

"Back to your place."

"I fell asleep early last night," I say. "He must have come in quiet and grabbed the bass."

"He can get freaky quiet."

I stand, and it occurs to me I might not be in this apartment again for a long time, if ever. I'll miss it, or maybe I'm just already missing those days when the Shits hung around here, lolled on the floor, dreamed of dark, impending relevance.

"What happened to us?" I say.

"Us?"

"The band."

"You don't know?" Hera says.

11

"I'm not sure."

"You were always a naive one."

"Really? But I'm the only one who's read Baudrillard."

"The Shits are the past," Hera says. "I have new outlets for my talent now. Thorazine takes up a lot of my spare time."

"All you have is spare time. Thorazine?"

"That's what Wallach and I are calling our new project."

"Jesus."

"It's a different thing, Jonathan. A different avenue of expression."

"Jack."

"Fine," Hera says. "I wish you the best, Jack."

Hera smiles that winning smile, the one full of wry kindness, which, along with her small trust fund, used to be our band's main bonding agent.

"What about Artaud's Garage?" I say.

"What about it?"

"We have a show next week."

"You're not hearing me. The Shits are over."

"I'm not going to let that happen, Hera. We've come too far."

"It's so strange to hear you say that. I don't believe we've come any distance at all."

"Only history can judge," I say. "Besides, what about that new song we wrote?"

"'Ghost Strap'? I'm actually giving that to Thorazine. It works better with Wallach."

"But I wrote the bass line," I say. "And the bridge."

"We're not using the bass line. We'll change the bridge."

"I came up with the phrase *Ghost Strap*."

"Those are just words," Hera says. "Words belong to every-body. Tell you what, though."

"What."

"As a favor? You find Alan and your bass and Cutwolf agrees, I'll play the Garage. One last show. A farewell performance."

"You will?"

"And then it's fuck the Shits. Fuck them forever."

Maybe Hera is right to move on. Bands, lovers, come, go. How long were the Beatles actually together? Or the original Murder Junkies?

I was in the Annihilation of the Soft Left for a year and a half before I started the Shits with Cutwolf and the Earl, though I was not a founding member of TAOTSL by any means. They were one of the most ancient bands on the scene, bitter elder statesmen (and, occasionally, stateswomen) who'd paid their dues back in the grimy agon of the '80s, when squatter blood dripped off cop batons in Tompkins Square Park and the crooked political pimps of the broken city sold New York's ass block by block to the fat-fuck real estate barons. Or at least that's how the band's songs explained it.

The Annihilation of the Soft Left had been through about seventeen players. The last original member was this seared crust of a dude with the *nom de rock* Toad Molotov. Some considered it a rite of passage to play in Toad's version of the band, to study at his combat boots, as it were, to listen to his harangues about—you guessed it—the soft left (or pretty much any polit-ical tendency that failed to snuggle up to his vague, often con-tradictory, but severely enforced ideology, once characterized

13

by Hera as "anarcho-bewildered"). To watch Toad munch a revolting quantity of his beloved mint-jelly sandwiches, swill Cuervo Gold, and scratch unrelentingly beneath his fatigue shorts at his hairy legs and crotch was to come of age in the rock underworld.

I apprenticed myself to Toad and learned the classic numbers: "Fire in Reagan's Urethra (Dishonorable Discharge)," "Mommy Got Screwed by the System (and Knocked Up with Me)," "Annihilate the Soft Left"—which Toad always reminded us was the band's mission statement, and so could be forgiven its melodic shortcomings. The songs were rousing in the briefest bursts and not very complicated. They were also remarkably similar. Toad said he'd written them in a single morning eleven years earlier, after ingesting something he referred to, with cryptic reverence, as a meth burrito.

The Banished Earl never played in TAOTSL but he used to hang around the band, and that's where I met him. Toad mentored the Earl, though Molotov was much more the Old Testament prophet, an Amos or Jeremiah, whereas the Earl gravitated toward some slacker-Byronic ideal. I think Toad wanted to politicize the Earl, activate him for revolutionist chaos, but that was a doomed dream. The Earl was too much the soul pirate, a rover upon womb-warm seas of introspection. That's why the dope suited him. It filled his sails, at least for a while. It's Doldrums City these days.

Anyway, the Earl used to sit around with the rest of us, listen to Toad lecture the room on the police state, the lessons of Bakunin, and why only a fuck javelin or a kulak would buy a Popsicle at the bodega when you could make them at home with a ninety-nine-cent can of Dole pineapple juice, Dixie cups, and some wooden toothpicks. But every so often the Earl and I would look at each other and he'd get this subversive glint in his eye, like he wasn't really buying Toad's rants and guessed that I wasn't either. I think we both knew our days in Toad's punk rock atelier were numbered, that soon it would be time to break with the old man, who was nearly thirty-four by then.

I dread the idea of seeing Toad again, and I doubt the Earl has squirreled himself away with our old sensei, but I have to make sure, head toward Toad's place near St. Marks. It's four o'clock in the afternoon, already dark. The bars and coffee shops beckon with their neon invitations to creature coziness, and I could really use a cup of java. But now is no time to dawdle. I press on.

Snowflakes flutter in the brittle air, burst in freezing kisses on my face.

Truth is, despite our roots in the Annihilation of the Soft Left, the Shits are pretty soft ourselves. We are not from the streets. We are each of us semi-misfits from one middle-class suburb or another, except for Hera, who hails from serious money. Her father is one of those junk bond guys, almost went to jail. The rest of us are usually broke, but there are family basements with foldout couches flung across the American empire (New Jersey for me, Long Island for the Earl, Ohio for Cutwolf) for us to flee to in case of utter collapse. These are couches of last resort.

The Shits are pretty left-wing, I guess, but our irony smothers our politics.

I know this makes the older types crazy. It made Toad nuts. People think we have no beliefs. Trust me, we do. They're just tiny, fuzzy, fragile things, like fresh-born chicks. We do all we can to protect them, to feed them plump, life-sustaining kitsch worms and keep those greedy killers, the fucking baby boomers, at bay.

Besides, what exactly are *their* beliefs? Dancing to the worst Fleetwood Mac song while balloons float down from the rafters?

I once wrote a song for Toad about a certain breed of former flower person. It was called "Deadhead Fuck," and it went like this:

> *Deadhead hippie fuck*
> *Livin' on the corporate suck*
> *Out of time, out of luck*
> *Deadhead hippie fuck*

Toad vetoed the tune. Said it was too obvious. This from the man who wrote "Intercontinental Ballistic Butt Plug (in Caspar Weinberger's Butt)."

Still, he had a point. Protest songs are not my strong suit. I may not have a strong suit. But I do possess a willingness to flash-freeze my testicles on this desperate quest to reclaim my Fender and save the Shits from oblivion. That should count for something.

I lean on Toad's buzzer, but there is no answer.

It's too cold to linger. I head across the street to the Pinsk Diner, order a coffee, scratch out a potential set list for next week's show on a napkin:

The Man Went Out
Spores
Invention of the Shipwreck
Orbit City Comedown
Ghost Strap

Bag Fever (Ain't Gonna Break)
Orange Julius Rosenberg
Horst with No Name

"Hey, you're in that band."

I look up at the woman on the stool beside me. She's about my age, wears a crinkly polyester nurse's uniform, her greasy hair pinned back with plastic barrettes. Her wide face and insect-green eyes look familiar.

"Who wants to know?" I say.

"Me."

"And who are you supposed to be? A nurse?"

"If you're a lumberjack," she says, points to the thermal sleeve that pokes past the cuff of my work shirt.

"It's called layering," I say.

I remember this woman from a show a few months ago at the Knitting Factory, a club the Shits will one day conquer. A band from Louisville played, acid punk, somewhat algebraic. She stood near the front in the same dress, did this alluring, slightly spasmodic dance, a sequence of languid shudders.

"I'm Corrina," she says. "I've seen you guys."

"Where?"

"At the Spiral. In the basement."

"Oh, right. We opened for Vole."

"You were . . . I thought it was brave."

"Thanks."

"You guys don't care about all the bullshit."

"Which bullshit?"

"Like notes and stuff."

"We have a philosophy."

"I can tell. I'm into it."

"Cool. I'm Jonathan."

"Hi, Jonathan."

"I mean, Jack," I say.

"Okay, Jack."

"I changed my name. To Jack Shit."

"Just now?"

"Yesterday."

"Gotcha."

"Because that's my band. The Shits."

"Oh, you're in the Shits?"

"Yeah, what did you think?"

"I don't know. I just remembered seeing your band. Not the name."

Corrina slurps up the last of her borscht, tugs an intricately folded piece of green paper from a vinyl coin pouch.

She holds up what looks like a duck, peels it open into a five-dollar bill, smooths it out on the counter.

"I call it money-gami."

I laugh.

"What's so funny?"

"Nothing."

"I can sell you one."

"How much?"

"Seven bucks."

"For a fiver?"

"For a one."

"How much for a five?"

"Five."

"That doesn't make any sense."

"That's because you're thinking about the money. Not the object."

"I have to think about the money. I only have a little bit until my next shift."

"At the lumberyard?"

"What? No, I work for a plant service, and sometimes I do phone surveys. Other stuff too. Dishwashing, or whatever I can find."

"Well, good luck, Jack Shit. Stay warm."

Corrina slides into her parka and leaves the Pinsk. I swivel on my stool, watch her through the big booth windows. The snow has picked up. Corrina unlocks an old Huffy bicycle, pushes off into the flurries.

I have some of my mother's old records, including Big Joe Turner singing "Corrine, Corrina." I wonder if the fake nurse has heard it. This false woodsman would like to play it for her.

There was always some kind of music in our house, though nobody played an instrument. When my mother did her calisthenics in that lavender leotard on our shag rug, made side three of the Rolling Stones' *Hot Rocks* skip on our Fisher turntable with every squat thrust, the sounds rainbowed out of the speakers, poured into me. Bill Wyman's bass bobbed up my gullet and locked in with Charlie Watts's snare, Keith's magpie shards of glinting guitar, and the mythic fibbing of Mr. Jagger.

"What can a poor boy do, except sing for a rock-and-roll band!" I screeched along with Mick.

"He's not a poor boy," my mother said, her legs up now for bicycles. "And he went to the London School of Economics."

Who knew what the hell that was, but it didn't sound like a place for a street-fighting man. Later my mother and father would point out the academic achievements of other noted musicians. Lou Reed studied poetry at Syracuse. That guy from the band Boston went to MIT, where he developed several important guitar pedals. (Too bad their music was overproduced tripe.) Even the Lizard King, Jim Morrison, majored in film at UCLA. Chuck D, as my father discovered in a newspaper article he clipped and presented to me last Thanksgiving, had met Flavor Flav at Adelphi University, not that my old man knew any songs by Public Enemy.

I guess I got the hint, because I did get a degree before I devoted myself to hard, spare modes of sonic expression, to the perpetuation and refinement of a radical stance vis-à-vis the rock mainstream, and to my personal dream of seriously bitching out on my bass guitar before an assembly of my punk and post-punk and art noise near-wave peers.

I throw a buck on the Pinsk counter and head down the avenue. The snow slants in harder, leaves a thin, slick coat on the sidewalk. Nobody is out here except a bundled-up old woman who sells clean needles from a fanny pack. The Earl calls her Our Lady of the Sealed Works. I've steered clear of that particular drug delivery system, except for once or twice, but maybe she's seen me with the Earl, a steady customer, because she nods as I walk past.

Sometimes I wonder why the Earl fell so hard for the heavy stuff and I didn't. I guess it's partly how we're wired. I did, a few months ago, dally with a glaringly unenviable speed-lord lifestyle, but I've sworn off powders since then. I also tried junk a few times before that. After the requisite upchuck, it felt exactly like the songs said it would. But something in me resisted the sensation. I didn't quite trust the warm cradle of it. Too much abyss underneath. It reminded me of an older, hollowed-out sadness, my bedroom water-stain year. Now I stick with beer and whiskey. Maybe booze rots you even worse over time, but at least I can I drink and still stay upright enough to tend to the Earl, our band, my sporadic employment.

When I get to my building there's a note scrawled on loose-leaf glued with chewing gum to the vestibule door: *Hit the Pit. C-Wolf.*

I crumple up the paper, turn back to the street. Somewhere in this polis of frozen stone are my bass and my bandmate. Perhaps they are together, perhaps apart. Either way, I must find them, save them.

THREE

The Stop Pit is really the Pit Stop. Hera just called it the Stop Pit by mistake one day and it stuck. The wooden bar is splintered and chipped, the mirror smeared, the stools scarred, crooked. It's that kind of dark, quasi-cheerful scuzz parlor where the outside world just desists for a while, and if you stay too long your life might also come to a gentle, oblivious halt. The Stop Pit, true to its true name, is crammed with checkered flags and faded photos of bygone mustachioed gods of the stock car circuit. Part of a grimed engine block dangles, chained, from the ceiling.

What a NASCAR honky-tonk is doing at Second and Second in the East Village might be anybody's guess, except we don't have to guess, we know. The place belongs to Hod Humphries, who played guitar in the proto-cowpunk combo the Saddle Sores, a legendary fixture at Max's Kansas City. The theme of the bar honors his hometown, Bristol, Tennessee, and its famous track, Bristol International Raceway, otherwise known as Thunder Valley.

Not that Cutwolf and I care about any of that, though Hod and his wife, Trancine, also late of the Saddle Sores, are sweet enough.

"Hi, kids," Trancine says now, sets us up with shots of rail rye and stubby Buds.

"Hey, Lady T," Cutwolf says. "New ink?"

Trancine's plump arms are sleeved in tattoos, swirls of Japanese dragons, cloud-wreathed pagodas. She holds out her wrist to show us her newest, a bright, dainty creature shiny with Vaseline.

"It's a fire belly newt."

"Beautiful," says Cutwolf.

I don't have any tattoos. Never wanted any. Cutwolf, who has a tattoo on his calf of a tattoo artist inking a baby cow on somebody's lower leg, says I have no visual sensibility. I told him I could see his point.

"You kids got any shows coming up?"

"Artaud's next week, if we aren't broken up."

"Ah, band tension. Don't miss that. Well, maybe me and Hod will make it out, though we don't go to clubs much anymore. Hod's fucked with his tinnitus. Wear earplugs, kids."

"Of course," I say.

We never do.

"Good. Hey, this round's on me."

Trancine taps the bar with her knuckles, moves off.

"Fire in the hole," I say.

Cutwolf and I down our shots, sip our beers. I fill him in on the Earl situation. The TV over the bar is hooked up to a VCR looping clips of vicious speedway crashes.

"Why would anybody even do that?" Cutwolf says, tilts his head up at the screen.

"I don't know. Why would anybody steal his bandmate's bass?"

"For drug money?"

"But why?" I say.

"Because drugs feel good? Ask the Earl."

"I would if I could find him."

"What did Hera say?"

"Hasn't seen him since last night."

"Was he high?"

"Apparently."

"You try Toad's?" Cutwolf asks.

"Wasn't answering."

"Dude's probably passed out with a mint-jelly sammitch in his paw."

We both grin at the image. Or at least that's why I grin. I'm not certain about Cutwolf. He could be recalling a deeply satisfactory bowel movement for all I know. Other minds are mysteries.

"Probably is," I say.

"Fuck, man," Cutwolf says, picks at the label on his bottle. Somebody told me that in Czechoslovakia, which I read in a *Newsweek* I found lying around the Pinsk has just become two separate countries, there is a crisp, delicious pilsner also called Budweiser, and that the Czechs and the Slovaks think our Budweiser tastes like crotch sweat. They may be right, but it's also a fact that Communism has fallen and it's the end of history, according to the same magazine. Who knows what's true? I read enough books in college to know that the truth is not really the point. My professors said that decentering thought and liberating it from the phallogocentric hegemony was the point. They are probably right, just like the Czechs and the Slovaks are right about our crap suds.

"What's that?" Cutwolf says now. "Suds?"

"Oh, nothing."

"Fucking Earl," Cutwolf says. "Why does he have to be such a dumb junkie?"

"Part of his curse."

"Curse? Fuck that. Guy has everything."

What Cutwolf means, I think, and all he ever means when he says stuff like this, is that the Earl is lucky to be such a natural beauty. Cutwolf and I are average-looking guys, not hideous, though I'm nearly a fat dude, will probably someday be a straight-up lard merchant, and Cutwolf has this cold, hollowed-out, drifter-killer look that would be more attractive without his weird habit of leveling a death stare at you even while remarking upon the weather. It's unsettling until you get used to it, though I haven't, not really.

Sometimes I wonder if Cutwolf experiences the same mixture of pride and pain that I do out on the street with the Banished Earl, all eyes sucking up our front man's luster. If we were horses, which I happen to know a little bit about from a fifth-grade research project, I'd be a Clydesdale (harnessed to one of the Budweiser wagons!), Cutwolf would be a spirited, maybe mildly diseased mustang, and Hera would be one of those impressive dressage horses, a Lipizzaner, strutting with handsome precision. But the Earl, he'd be the best the species has to offer, an Arabian. He'd gallop along the shoreline, ocean spray dancing around his flared nostrils, his fine stallion muscles heaving like the sea itself under his glistening coat.

I once ventured this analogy with Hera.

"Sounds like you want to fuck him," she said.

I turned away, stung.

"Why would I want to fuck a horse?" I said.

Anyway, it's painful to be a human sidecar to the Earl, who, even strung out on dope, unbathed, seems to fire the carnal furnaces of all who pass him on the avenue, though maybe in this neighborhood his stench, his opiated nodding, only add to the sex magic.

Nobody much notices the likes of Cutwolf and me. But at least we can each declare ourselves his buddy, which is more than you, for example, a passerby brought to boner or labial thrum by the corporeal splendor of the Earl, could ever hope to claim.

That's the pride part.

The Earl himself never seems much interested in the attention, which drives Cutwolf to a particular madness. Still, Cutwolf and I can only picture, and sometimes speculate aloud, what kinds of erotic quests we'd undertake if granted a day with our front man's visage and frame. But as I said, the Earl does not take advantage of his genetic fortune, which I guess lies at the core of Cutwolf's ire. For as long as I've known him, the Earl has pledged himself to only two loves, the one human, name of Hera, the other a substance derived from the latex of the breadseed poppy, both known often enough as "H."

Cutwolf goes to the toilet and I watch Daytona wreckage pile up on the TV. The bar's grown crowded and somebody hovers over the empty stool beside me.

"Hi again. Is this taken?"

It's Corrina, the woman from the Pinsk. I'm not shocked. These streets are a tiny town if you hardly leave them.

"My friend's coming back."

"How are you sure?"

"He's that kind of guy."

"Leal?"

"What's leal?"

"Loyal."

"Kind of leal, then, I guess. More like limited options."

"Is he in your band?"

"He's the guitar player."

"What are you?"

"I thought you said you saw us."

"I did."

"You don't remember what I play?"

"I remember. You do this weird, funny hop when you perform."

"And you do a weird, funny twitch when you watch."

"I do?"

"It's good. Intense."

"Thanks. I'm sorry I can't remember your instrument. Definitely not drums. You have that cool girl drumming for you."

"Woman."

"Oh, sorry."

"Well, *you* can say it," I say.

"Yes, I can. Anyway, I know you weren't the singer. That was that stuck-up-looking foppish boy. Or man? But back to you and your instrument. I don't remember any keyboards. I'm going to guess . . . bass."

"Tell her what she's won."

"I knew it."

"Wait," I say. "What do you mean, stuck-up, foppish? The Earl?"

"The who?"

"Most people go crazy for him. Can't control themselves. Like he's a cross between Elvis and Marilyn Monroe. And an Arabian stallion."

"Is he Arabian?"

"He's Lebanese."

"I see the attraction. From a technical standpoint. But his looks are too obvious for me. I have different taste. Less conventional."

27

"Ogres like me are grateful such taste exists."

"Oh, no, you are definitely good-looking, just in a really lame, boring way."

"I am?"

"You seem pleased."

"It's the nicest thing I've heard in a while. Vesna used to say she was glad I didn't distract her with attractiveness."

"Who's Vesna?"

"Doesn't matter. She's gone."

Trancine comes over, drops a coaster in front of Corrina.

"Hey, honey. How are you?"

"Not too shabby. Talking to this aspiring musician here."

"You seen them?" Trancine says. "The Craps?"

"The Shits," I say.

"Right. The Craps were from my time. Sounded a little like the Cramps. Kind of a rip-off, in fact. But you guys are the Shits. You're good kids. Except maybe that singer. Oh, he's okay. Such a looker."

"Has he been in here?" I say.

"I haven't seen him. Ask Hod. So, Corrina. The usual?"

"Yes, please."

Trancine reaches for the Popov in the speed rack and a pitcher from the fridge, mixes Corrina a Bloody Mary.

"How's that husband of yours?" Trancine says.

"Which one?" Corrina says.

"Ha!" Trancine says, winks at me.

Corrina raises her highball glass.

"To my new friend, Jack," she says, takes a shallow sip.

Cutwolf shuffles out of the bathroom, still buttoning up his black jeans. He fastens his huge vintage rodeo buckle. Sometimes I worry he's going to bend over too quickly, gut himself on the brass horns. He glowers at Corrina, who sips her drink on what was formerly his stool.

"I'll go ask around about Alan," Cutwolf says. Perhaps he uses the Earl's given name to remind me of priorities. "I'll leave a note on your door if I hear anything."

"You can just call," I say. "I have a telephone, remember?"

This is mostly for Corrina's benefit. It's important that she knows I'm a person with resources, reach, even if I'm behind on the bill, on the verge of disconnection.

"Yeah, but your answering machine is still broken," Cutwolf says. "It clicks on but then clicks off and I waste my quarter."

Cutwolf does not have a home telephone, mostly because his home is a walled-off corner of an old storefront, an illegal sub-sublet. He also cherishes his quarters. Laundry and pinball are foundational components of his week.

"Okay," I say. "See you later."

Cutwolf slips out into the winter gloom.

"Going to hit the head," I say.

I'm not sure why I call it that, and Corrina gives me a funny look.

"My father used to say 'head,'" she says. "Were you in the navy?"

"Almost," I say, and I'm not sure why, except that I think it might impress her, and there's a steady dilation of something like enthrallment I'm experiencing in the vicinity of this fake nurse, though who's to say she's not also a real nurse? Thing is, I haven't even bothered to find out. My mother always told me that one of the many reasons men are despicable is because they'd rather cling to some fantasy version of the women in their lives than explore reality together. Not that I ever had a fantasy about health care imposters.

"By the way," I say. "Before I go. Are you a real nurse?"

"Not specifically. My mother is."

I head into the head, muse upon the linguistic glitch that allows me to say, *I'm heading into the head*, my mind also a churn of questions: Where is the Earl? Where is my bass guitar? Will the Shits ever play Barcelona? Is post-punk dead? Is the Earl? What is post-punk? Why does Corrina make me feel like I'm burning up and shivering at the same time? Her grasshopper eyes? Her terse smile? Her grease-shiny hair? Her medical fashions? The wisdom of a Bloody Mary?

I stand over the toilet bowl, lately vacated by Cutwolf, glimpse his thick, tarry offering to the sewers of New York City, the Stop Pit's water pressure apparently too weak to flush it. The turd that clogs the bowl looks born of great strain, not at all the issue of a man prone to grin in reminiscence of his most recent colonic event.

I hose a hard stream of piss into the heart of my bandmate's log, as though to laser it asunder, but fail to pierce the dark impaction.

I try to flush it, but the bowl brims with brown soup.

There is a knock at the door and I open it a crack.

Corrina leans her face in close to mine.

"I need to tell you something," she says.

"Yeah?"

Corrina sniffs the air, winces.

"It's not mine," I say.

"It's okay," she says, kisses me, a medium-long kiss with lip suck, lip nibble, tongue poke. It's the best and only kiss I've had for a while.

"Is that what you wanted to tell me?" I say.

"No," she says, plucks a ballpoint from her nonspecific fake-

30

nurse dress pocket, writes on my palm. It's an address, not far from here.

"Was that what you wanted to tell me?"

"No," she says, and kisses me again, this time a quick graze on the cheek. She stops, sniffs the air again, rears back.

"It's not me, I promise," I say.

"Okay," she says, leaves.

I turn back to the toilet, to the lake of dark sludge in the bowl, try to imagine what my musical forebears would have done after fouling the john of some goodly tavern keepers. Led Zeppelin, surely, would slink right out (as did Cutwolf, the actual fecalist), if not find a way to worsen the mess by dumping in a magnum of champagne, a platter of room service steaks. Johnny Rotten would sneer beneath his fiery hair, skulk off. G. G. Allin of the Murder Junkies would likely scoop out the deuce for a facial treatment. But the Clash, those large-hearted, collective-minded fellows, and Joe Strummer in particular, the diplomat's son, would they not clear the clog and mop the slop before heading off to an antiracism rally? This is my belief, anyway. I reach back behind the toilet tank, grab an old, crusted plunger, get to work, just another amateur plumber humming "Spanish Bombs."

When I'm done, I wash my hands in the cracked sink, walk back to the bar. I scan the room for Corrina on the off chance she's still here.

"She's a strange bird," Trancine says. "But a good egg."

"But which came first?" I say.

"Huh?"

"Nothing. What's her story?"

"Not sure. She comes in a lot."

"I come in a lot. I've never seen her."

31

"No?"

"Though maybe I have."

It's odd, but I now realize I *have* seen her before, and not just at the Pyramid, or the Spiral, or the Pinsk. My mind loads up a brand-new carousel of memory slides and she starts to appear all over the neighborhood, at bodegas and coffee shops and maybe even the Jew-Hater's bar, another Shits hangout, where the drinks are almost cheap enough to compensate for the old tap-puller's genocidal arias, and definitely here, in the Stop Pit.

"She's some kind of artist," Trancine says.

"Shocker."

"Sometimes I wish a stockbroker would just walk in here."

"Be careful what you wish for."

"I know what you mean. Man, the fucking rents are just rocketing. Guy who owns this building likes us, knows me and Hod from way back, but things are changing. People like you and your buddy Cutwolf are coming in droves."

"People like me and Cutwolf?"

"Don't take this wrong. Y'all are sweethearts, but you kids are pretty yuppie. Compared to what the neighborhood used to be."

"Hey," I say. "I'm just here to bitch out. It's my dream."

"Excuse me?"

"Lou Reed studied poetry at Syracuse, you know. It's not like he walked out of a salt mine."

"Lou Reed is a prick."

"He is?"

"Of course. I still love him. A salt mine?"

"Sure," I say.

"Whatever."

"Hey," I say. "Are you guys going to get any of that Slovakian Budweiser?"

"What is that?" Trancine says.

"It's the future," I say.

"Well, if it's the future, then I guess we'll be getting it. Can't change the future."

"You can't?"

"That's what makes it the future. If it doesn't happen, it's not the future."

"I'll have to think about that," I say.

"You do that, college boy."

FOUR

Home, I fry up some eggs for dinner. The radiator hisses in harmony with my sunnysides and I sweat hard at the stove in my boxers. Nobody can control the boiler in the basement. It's an all-or-nothing infernal machine.

There are not a lot of amenities here in the Rock Rook, unless you've always wanted your shower in the kitchen and find the company of cockroaches—our exoskeletal courtiers, as the Earl calls them—oddly calming. But you can't beat the rent, not around here.

I sit with my eggs, mop up yolk with a stale Dorito, read some *Our Lady of the Flowers* by Jean Genet. It's one of the Earl's favorites, along with *Daryl Hall/John Oates: Dangerous Dances* by Nick Tosches, and sometimes he'll read me sections of both books while I rehearse bass lines.

The Earl told me that *Flowers* was written by Genet in prison so he could have something to whack off to.

"That's the purest kind of literature," he said. "Otherwise you're just writing for money, or fame, or to look good."

"What about to make a better world?" I said.

"That's only ever a by-product. You can't set out that way. Otherwise it will be false, stilted. You write a book to jerk off to. If it's great, it will set people free."

"Free to jerk it."

34

"Jonathan, think of all the things you are not doing when you beat off. For that moment, at least, you're not killing, maiming, stealing, lying, cheating. You're not participating in the carnage of the system."

"You sound like Toad."

"Toad has blue balls. He could use a good tug."

"Isn't it better to make love with another person?"

"Is that what people make with each other?"

"I think so."

"I'll tell Hera."

The Earl chuckled, fell back into a light nod.

This conversation took place only months ago, but it feels like years.

Sometimes, when he lounged by the window in the late-afternoon light, the Earl acquired this heavenly shimmer. It was hard to picture him as he was onstage, a broiling demon, a louche god, a howling blues dog and ancient babyman and suave crooner, a society of the spectacle unto himself, a walking mirror phase, a simulacrum but also the return and revenge of the repressed desert of the real, never quite of us but our reason for being, or at least being together.

We've always believed in the Banished Earl more than in ourselves. That's why we went along with his idea for our names. He pilfered his and Cutwolf's from characters in a book by this Elizabethan gadfly named Thomas Nashe, a crumbly paperback called *The Unfortunate Traveler, or the Life of Jack Wilton.* The Earl found it tossed on some sidewalk trash heap, the same way he'd discovered *Our Lady* and *Dangerous Dances.* The Earl dropped out of community college, reads whatever the street proffers.

"And you, Jonathan," he said after one of our early band

practices, over shots of house bourbon at the Stop Pit. "You can just be Jonathan. Jonathan Shit. The standard-bearer."

"I'm staying Hera Bernberger," Hera said.

The Earl smiled.

"As anyone in their right mind would."

Without the Earl, we are a raucous, semi-coherent noise band. With him, we edge up to the portal of depraved magnificence.

I always figured that if we worked hard, played enough shows, wrote a few more songs as good as "Orbit City Comedown" or "Spores" or "Invention of the Shipwreck" or possibly even "Ghost Strap," we might stride through that portal. It's all I've wanted. Now, with Hera's desertion and the Earl's disappearance, I'm beginning to doubt everything. Most people surrender their dream long before they fly to Barcelona. They plan far in advance to give up, even if they don't know it. Maybe they seize on the dream in the first place to have something to quit, a failure they can point to, say, "See, I tried," and get on with their dismal lives.

Even Cutwolf's commitment seems shaky lately. Just the other day we were at the Laundromat, relaxing in those mustard-yellow hardshell chairs. We talked big picture, watched our jeans and skivvies spin.

"I'm just saying," Cutwolf said. "I need to think about other things. My uncle back in Ohio makes good money tiling fancy kitchens and bathrooms. I could work for him and look into grad school. I don't want to be thirty years old and still in a band."

"Why not? I want to be in a band when I'm fucking eighty. What's wrong with that? Look at Suicide. Alan Vega is my dad's age."

"I know. But it just seems kind of sad."

"Sad? Sad is all that maturity bullshit. Going to school. Training to be a drone. If you're lucky."

"Life is not just a choice between the Shits and being a drone."

"What if it is?" I said, to which Cutwolf had no reply.

When I relayed this conversation to the Earl, he chuckled, rancorless but dismissive, as though he floated above such petty anxieties, which he did, usually with the aid of various powders.

"Don't worry, Jonathan," he said. "Whatever happens will not only happen but has already happened, in all possible ways."

There is deep Zen clarity in this idea, but it's not necessarily the answer to everything, and I told the Earl as much.

"There is no answer to everything," he said.

"But what if Cutwolf quits the band?"

"I'll learn bass. You'll switch to guitar."

"You think the bass is that easy?"

"No, Jonathan. But I think you will make a good teacher."

Recalling this compliment makes me miss the Earl. I see him lost, wandering some frozen hinterland like in those Russian novels from my world lit class, and I hope he's okay, but I'm beginning to suspect he may be far, very far—many fucking versts, in fact—from the province of okay.

The Earl has filched my stuff for dope money before, including compact discs, records, and a pleather car coat of which I was quite fond, but I always considered these minor crimes, nothing compared to the gift he bestowed on all of us with his presence, his pledge, when it came to our shows, to leave everything out on the bitching floor.

Sometimes his squirrelly drug-fiend behavior grates, but I

guess until now I couldn't face the gravity of his situation, his disease.

Steal a roommate's favorite jacket or scratched *Trout Mask Replica* LP, that's one thing. To take your bandmate's only working instrument, that's just the ultimate sacrilege, born of a sickness heretofore unknown.

FIVE

The next morning Dyl Becker from King Snake Guitars calls, whispers over the line.

"Jonathan."

"Jack."

"Sorry. Jack."

"What is it, Dyl? Why are you whispering?"

"I'm in the bathroom. There's a guy here at the store. He's got your bass. He's trying to sell it to me."

"Holy shit. Who is he?"

"I don't know. Never seen him before. Doesn't really seem like a musician."

"You sure it's mine?"

"It doesn't have the Annihilation sticker, but I can see the outline of it."

"Fuck, Dyl. Stall him. I'll be right over."

Not quite ten minutes later, I push through the King Snake door, stamp the slush off my sneakers. It's a narrow shop, the pegged walls lined with dozens of guitars, some vintage, others just used, electrics and acoustics, Gibsons, Fenders, Martins, and an antique metal-bodied National resonator with a biscuit bridge. Winter light beams through the glass storefront, catches the finish on a gorgeous Les Paul Goldtop that hangs on the wall behind the counter. Cutwolf plays a snazzy mint-green SG but drools whenever he sees this particular Gibson, maybe secretly pictures himself the second coming of Jimmy Page, sawing on the strings with a violin bow, blouse cuffs flopped over his hands. Not very punk, technically speaking, but I've cut back on the puritanism. Many roads lead to the Shits. Also, though they should be condemned for their rockist excesses both personal and aesthetic, as well as for their hypothetical indifference to the Stop Pit's plumbing crisis, the Zep did slay.

I spot Dyl behind the counter. He looks nervous beneath his springy coils of Twinkie-yellow hair. His eyes dart to mine past the immense form that looms before him, a punishing-looking white dude with a massive Easter Island head, a long silver braid, a purple leather duster. My J-Bass is a toy in his huge, puffy hands.

"J-Jack," Dyl says, and I'm not sure if he stutters because he's scared or because he's still getting used to my new name. "Funny you should walk in just now. This gentleman here, he was inquiring about selling this bass. I was just explaining how we would need papers for that."

"Papers are bullshit," the man says. His thick voice seems to gurgle up from a phlegm font in his chest. "Just give me three hundred bucks. It's a nice guitar."

"It *is* a nice guitar," I say. "Looks like a nineteen-seventy-five four-bolt Fender Jazz with pearl inlays. Really sweet."

"Lucky me," the man says. His slate eyes stare down, his smooth face taut with the cold wisdom of lizards.

"And unlucky me," I say.

"Oh, yeah? Why's that?"

Behind the giant, Dyl shakes his head. I guess he figures I

should let this slide. But what's the guy going to do? He moves on me, I'm out the door. My only worry is he'll drop the bass, put a crack in the neck. He could, of course, put a crack in Dyl's neck. But Dyl knew the risks when he took a job in a music store.

"I said why's that?" the guy says. "Why unlucky you?"

"Because that's my bass."

"Excuse me?"

"I don't know how you got it, and I'm not saying you stole it, but that's my bass guitar."

"The hell it is."

"Dyl, is that the case open on the counter?"

"It's what he brought it in."

"Red velvet interior," I say, "with two cigarette burns near the center. Thank you for that, Hera Bernberger. Oh, and are both latches loose? Thing is always flipping open."

"Yep," Dyl says.

"And is there a distortion pedal in there. A Pro Co Rat? My initials are on the side. In white. I wrote them with correction fluid."

"It's here," Dyl says, holds up my Rat, a small black box with three knobs and a silver foot switch. It's the only effect I ever use. Cutwolf favors the MXR Distortion Plus. We are both minimal when it comes to gear. We have a one-pedal rule.

The big man cranes his head back to the counter, looks over at me, shrugs.

"Possession is nine-tenths of the law," he says, and I'm surprised such a hard guy would resort to a phrase that bullies used to toss around in the schoolyard to justify swiping some kid's Jolly Ranchers.

"Sir," I say, "that may be true. But may I ask how it came into your possession?"

"I'm a musician. I bought it a long time ago."

"And what sort of music do you play?"

The man grins.

"You know, rock 'n' roll, baby! The punk jams and shit. The latest grooves for the kids with the safety pins in their tits."

"Okay," I say. "You're about fifteen years too late on that, but what bands are you into?"

"Bands?"

"Yeah."

"You mean what groups do I like?"

"Yes."

Maybe it's risky to push him like this, but I can't stand to see my beloved fish in his hands.

"Well," he says. "I really like the Go Fuck Yourself."

"Don't think I know them," I say.

"They're fantastic. I'm also partial to the Walk Away Now Before I Rip Out Your Spinal Cord and Run It Up Your Ass Trio."

"Oh," I say. "Are they a trio now?"

"That's right." The giant smirks. "Tighter sound."

"Jack," Dyl says, "I don't think this guy is messing."

"Your shaggy amigo is correct. Your name is Jack?"

"That's Jack Shit," Dyl says. "From the Shits."

"Is it now? Jack Shit. That's your real name?"

"It's my stage name."

"You'll go far."

"Thanks."

"So, let me ask you something. If this is your guitar, as you say, can you show me the papers? The bill of sale this dipstick keeps going on about?"

"Jack, just show him."

"I don't have it," I say. "I don't know where it is."

"Jesus, Jack," Dyl says. "You've really got to have the papers."

"Yeah, Jack," the man says. "Get your act together."

"It's still my bass," I say. "Did the Earl trade it to you for dope?"

"Dope? Do I look like a drug dealer?"

Dyl and I exchange glances.

"Okay, I'll give you that. What is it? The coat?"

"And the braid," Dyl adds. "The two together."

"Interesting. And I guess this can't hurt."

The giant tugs back his duster, reveals the New York Islanders jersey underneath.

"A hockey shirt?" Dyl asks.

"No, you stupid fuck. *This*."

The man draws a knife from a sheath strapped to his waist. It's long, jagged, black.

"Genuine Gerber combat blade," he says. "We used it in the forces when we trained in Filipino edged weapon systems. Completes the look, right?"

"Ah, definitely," Dyl says, in a quiet voice.

"Actually," I say, "a gun would fit the profile better. Like a TEC-9."

"TEC-9. Where you'd hear that? TV?"

"A rap song."

"Hilarious. Okay, you got me. I'm not really a drug dealer. I mean, I know some. And I admire them. Their business acumen. But I do other kinds of work. When I'm not pumping out the hot new-wave tunes. You guys dig Bachman-Turner Overdrive?"

The giant waves his blade.

"They had an undeniable pop sensibility," Dyl says. "And a decent second- or third-tier hard rock guitar sound."

"That's so fucking generous of you," the man says, and looks about to carve up poor Dyl, but the front door jingles and in walks the Denim Ghoul, my pal from the pizza joint. The Ghoul shivers in his thin jacket, his bare belly wrinkled and concave beneath his mesh half-shirt. He holds aloft a plastic baggie full of nine-volt cells.

"You guys buy used batteries?" he says.

The giant sheathes his blade, pulls his coat shut, slips my bass back into its velveteen cradle. I wonder if he means to leave it, but he closes the case, swings it off the counter.

"Jack Shit," he says, shakes his head. "You kids think it's so provocative, all this mama, papa, caca, pee-pee. But it's just diaper rash. Hey, that's not a bad name for a band. Diaper Rash. You like it?"

"Definitely," Dyl says, frightened, perhaps, into permanent affirmation.

"Don't lie to me. I know it's dumb. All right, I'm going now. Sorry we couldn't do business. Maybe you could have helped your buddy, too."

"My buddy?" I say.

"Alan. Your good pal, Alan."

"You know where he is?"

"It's not for me to say."

"What does that mean?"

"It means, b-b-b-baby, you ain't seen nothing yet!"

The big man pushes out of King Snake. I move to follow but the Denim Ghoul snatches my arm.

"Let him go," the Ghoul says.

His bony grip is strong.

"He knows where my friend is," I say. "He has my bass."

"Bide your time," the Ghoul says. "Be very careful."

"You know that guy?"

"Mounce? Yes, I know him. He's a killer. He's killed more than a few of us, you know."

The Denim Ghoul releases me, squeezes my shoulder, almost avuncular, heads out into the street with his batteries.

"That bastard called him Alan," I say to Dyl. "That's bad news. The Earl hates his name. He would only give it up under serious duress."

"What the fuck is going on, Jack?" Dyl says, with a tinge of his trademark whine. It's not one of those counterintuitively seductive whines. It lacks the subtle nasal insouciance, for instance, of certain strains of punk declaimers, or even Dyl's namesake, Mr. Zimmerman. Dyl's whine is just flustered, annoying. But he's a decent guy, and I don't hold it against him, even if he'll never be a Shit. He looks about ready to weep as he fidgets with some humbuckers on the counter.

"I don't really know what's going on," I say.

"Is it like a kidnapping?"

"Maybe. But has anyone been contacted? I'd know if anybody had called the Earl's folks."

"Maybe he's into the dealers for money."

"He usually just cops from the street, a bag or two at a time. He can't have racked up that kind of debt. The kind that brings in a guy like—what was his name? Mounce?"

"What about what that homeless dude said? About how Mounce or whatever killed a lot of them?"

"Dyl, how do you know he's homeless?"

"I mean . . ."

45

"You're just assuming that. You have no idea where he sleeps."

"Sorry."

"It's okay. I was thinking about that comment too. I don't know what he meant. We need to talk to somebody who's been around here longer than us."

"Like Toad."

"Maybe he's home now. Or awake."

"Or maybe we should just call the police."

"I definitely have mixed feelings about that."

Dyl nods. He understands. It's not that I hate the five-0 categorically, though my days under Toad Molotov's tutelage fostered in me an intense dislike for the institution of law enforcement insofar as its function is to protect the property of the rich and repress all resistance to the tyranny of the transnational order, not to mention assault and incarcerate all who fail to conform to the prescribed American lifestyle, namely that of a brainwashed consumer of corporate foodstuffs and folkways.

But that's not why I'm loath to dime the fuzz.

The real reason is more personal.

SIX

A few months ago, when I veered into that speed jag, I kind of came unhinged. I'd snort mounds of this wretched bodega stuff that smelled and tasted of the scouring powder they probably cut it with, sit on my foam mat and grind my teeth for eight- or ten-hour stretches. I'm not really sure how it started, but an inner civilizational decline had begun even before I started in with the nose Comet.

Vesna had finally broken it off after an admittedly poor showing on my part, such as the several occasions when I'd call her to say I was coming over and then just start in with heavy bong work and listen to records with the Earl and forget. Or else I'd get drunk, pester her for sex, prove myself too limp for anything but needy cuddles. Worse, I'd launch into endless soliloquies about the aesthetic trajectory of the Shits and the meaning of our songs within the context of the last seventy years of Western cultural production. I was just that sort of pedantic knob my mother had begged me not to emulate (when she wasn't insisting I emulate no man who ever existed), and Vesna, who was smart and mature and worked in a real office helping homeless people (hence my probably self-serving display of ire at Dyl's assumptions about the Denim Ghoul's residential status), deserved better, and one day woke to that very revelation.

She dumped me over a plate of pierogi at the Pinsk.

I dragged ass for weeks after that, could barely remember my bass parts at band practice. I couldn't cut it at my jobs, either, one of which was at a sprawling phone farm on Canal Street where we cold-called poor slobs across the nation to ask them questions about donuts, abortion, basketball, car insurance, or whatever else our clients requested. You got paid, beyond the paltry base salary, by the completed survey, and I was averaging about none a week. My supervisor, Mr. Ramos, threated to can me, which would leave me with just my part-time plant-watering gig.

The Earl had mentioned in passing these little wax pouches of powder they were selling cheap at the bodega, one of those corner stores where you can deduce the true nature of their business plan by the visible inventory: one sun-faded box of Tide, a rack of stale Hubba Bubba, a few loose Pepsis.

After being asked more than once if I was a cop by the man behind the bulletproof plastic and wondering if I'd receive better service if I answered in the affirmative, I eventually got my hands on Manhattan's crappiest street drugs. I figured I'd limit myself to sparing bumps, just enough to motivate me to rejoin the world. I'd nail down my bass parts, crank out the surveys, reconstitute myself as a viable and generous sex option. I'd win back the affections of both Mr. Ramos and Vesna.

But for some reason it didn't quite work that way. In lieu of a triumphant reentry into semi-vigorous living, I found myself stuck in a jittery rut. I'd either rock catatonically on the foam mat or stare through the front door peephole in a state of brain-flensing paranoia. This stuff was not the so-called meth burrito of Toad Molotov's compositional golden hour. I couldn't have written a shopping list on this shit.

The only person I'd ever see was the Earl, who'd come and go with dependable adherence to his junkie Dracula routines. Vlad the Self-Impaler. He'd nod to me as I clutched my knees and twitched on my mat, retire to his plywood sarcophagus. I stopped going to work and practice, stopped showering because I believed baby rats lived in the hem of the plastic shower curtain (why else would it ripple of its own accord like that?). I pretty much stopped eating, too, which for a devoted trencherman was surely a sign of doom.

I'm not exactly sure how long it went on like this, though I guess not long enough for all of the drug-and-booze-striated freaks in my social milieu to notice my disappearance and worry. Still, it went on for a while. All I did was sit on the mat, stand at the peephole, or venture out to the bodega for another yellow pouch of green-flecked funless crazy flakes.

At some point, the voices started. They drifted in through the open window. What I heard, or thought I heard, were the voices of the neighborhood, the demotic chorus. They sang of me.

"Yeah, man, he's up in that apartment right there just snorting his ass off."

"Ramos at the phone survey outfit really put his hand out. And that Jonathan just spat in it."

"Look at how he treated Vesna. Kept blowing her off so he could talk about Wire or the Birthday Party all night with his smacked-out boyfriend. Couldn't fuck her either. *Maricón.*"

"Yo, he can't stay up there forever, man."

"No shit."

"Don't matter. Word is out. The DA's put in the fucking paperwork. Narco squad's suiting up for the raid. J-dog is history. They'll get him on everything. Not just the drugs. They'll get him on the drinking. The loutish, male-chauvinist behavior. The gentrifying. Old stuff too. Possession of next week's Algebra II test with intent to distribute. Unlawful dissemination of cum stains on his mother's chaise longue. Breach of friendship. Misrepresentation of live music attendance."

"He didn't see the Gun Club when he was sixteen."

"No shit."

"Never even served in the Kiss Army."

"He's going away."

"True dat, homes."

"Word to your progenitor."

"Let it be a lesson. Kid can't even play. Fake-ass musician. One of these weak suburban fools thinks jumping around and stomping on that distortion pedal will disguise the fact that he knows fuck-all about his instrument, or music in general, outside one narrow little corner of Anglo-Saxon angst."

"Good riddance."

The precinct house was just a few blocks from my apartment. I don't quite remember the moment I rose from the mat and walked over there, but I recall the shock of the raw November air, the stale warmth of the station. I was coated with grime beneath the button-down shirt I'd donned for the occasion. People slid past me in the vestibule, pinched their noses.

The desk sergeant had a high, wood-paneled perch, a salt-and-pepper prog-rock mustache. He peered down like some feudal sheriff bored by the ceaseless plaints of villagers.

"Yeah?" he said.

I stared up, said nothing.

"How may I be of service, young man?"

"I'm here," I said.

"So it would seem."

"No, officer," I said. "It's me, Jonathan. The one you've been after? I'm here, okay? It's over. It's done, man. I'm done hiding."

"Excuse me?"

"No more games."

"Okay."

"Here I am, sir. Nice of me, right? Saving you the trip."

"The trip where?"

"I said no more games. Please, officer. I'm tired. Of the whole damn thing. I can't keep it up. I'm turning myself in. Just put on the fucking cuffs!"

Now the sergeant's face hardened, and I suppose it occurred to him that despite appearances I could be the real thing, a dangerous perp who'd made crime pay until some telltale palpitations sent me running to the pokey for punishment, and maybe absolution.

He stepped down from his desk, led me to a wooden bench. We sat together and the sergeant laid a large notebook with a soft leather sleeve on his knee.

"So, what's your name?"

"Jonathan."

"Jonathan what?"

"Well . . . in my world I'm known as Jonathan Shit."

The sergeant's pen hovered.

"And what about in this world?"

I recall a surge of resentment, a desire to debate this man on the definition of terms. But the moment passed and the surge splashed back into a thin, sour puddle in my gut.

"Liptak. Jonathan Liptak."

"And what did you do, Jonathan?"

"What?"

"Why is the NYPD after you?"

"You already know that. Jesus. Why are you mocking me?"

The sergeant wet his fingers, tamped down his mustache.

"Okay, fine. Maybe I do know. But I want to make sure we didn't miss anything. Better to get it all out in the open now. Don't you agree?"

"Yes, that's what I've been trying to say."

"Good. So, Jonathan, tell me, have you hurt anyone?"

"Vesna."

"What did you do to . . .Vesna?"

"I said . . . I promised . . ."

"Yeah?"

"I blew her off, okay? I listened to records instead."

"I see."

"Lost track of the time."

"Jonathan, have you physically harmed anyone?"

"Huh? No."

"Have you stolen anything?"

"No. Not since middle school. I stole Desmond Pellegrin's Chewbacca figurine."

"Okay. So, what's the deal here?"

"What do you mean?"

"Did you commit mail fraud?"

"No."

"Just a joke. Look, Jonathan. I need you to confess your crime. The hell you're in, it will never end unless you talk to me. What have you done?"

"I've done speed."

"Pardon?"

"I did a lot of shitty bodega speed. I was telling myself it was

coke but there is no way that stuff is coke. I've done other drugs
in the past. A lot of pot. I spent two months of college stoned
twenty-four-seven, watching reruns of *Miami Vice*."

"Okay."

"One time, Rico and Sonny find this rich kid OD'd in
a bathtub. Rico says, 'The saddest thing is an uptown junkie.
They're only into it because they hurt so much inside.' But that
bothered me. I mean, isn't that why all junkies are into it? Why
just the uptown ones? Seemed, I don't know, classist. I wouldn't
expect Tubbs to be that obtuse."

"Me neither."

"I'm sure you guys know this already, but once in high
school I got really stoned and drove home from my friend An-
drew's house. I came to this stop sign and just froze. It's three in
the morning, nobody around, and I just hang out there at the
stop for like forty minutes. Couldn't commit to the turn. I've
done other stuff. I come off as a pretty decent, dependable guy
but I know I can be passive-aggressive and a little cruel sometimes. I fought with my mom a lot when I was younger. Gave
her a lot of grief. I'm not a scumbag when it comes to girls, or,
I mean, women. My mom taught me a lot about how they've
had it rough. I get it. I'm a feminist. But still, sometimes I think
I'm kind of sleazy on the inside because there are times when
all I think about is—"

"Jonathan."

"What?"

"Stop."

"Okay."

"Are you high right now?"

"I wouldn't call it high. But if your question is am I on
drugs, the answer would be yes."

The sergeant stood, snapped his notebook shut.

"Yesterday we found a kid in a garbage can. Throat cut. You know anything about that?"

"Why would I?"

"He was a dumbass downtown white-boy garbagehead."

"We don't all necessarily know each other," I said.

"Okay, Jonathan. Jonathan Shit. I'm going back to my desk. I've got some work to do. I'm going to need you to sit here for a while."

"For how long?"

"For how long? Well, I'd like you to sit here for as long as it takes for it to really dawn on you where you are and what exactly you have been doing for the last twenty minutes. Once that sinks in, you are free to go. And don't worry about thanking me later. I'd love to never see your fucking face again."

I sat on that bench and it did all dawn on me. What dawned on me was that I was a major moron, that the cops weren't after me, and that nobody in this city, apart from maybe my band and Dyl, thought about me at all. Even to followers of the Shits, the few dozen who confessed to such a status, I was just the bassist, the afterthought. The cops were not organizing a manhunt. I guess I preferred that delusion to the truth: nobody fucking cared.

I hadn't noticed the shift change, but now a new sergeant sat behind the desk. His mustache was more handlebar. He winked down at me. He'd been briefed.

I felt weak, scooped out, but my mind was clear. I stood, walked out into the sunshine. It was the same cold autumn day, but brighter. I bought an egg cream at Gem Spa, took it to Tompkins Square Park. Dyl, out walking his dog, spotted me. I told him everything. I haven't touched any powders since. But

I still see no reason to talk to the cops. Not until we have no other choice. Besides, why would they care? They've probably got my name in a file: local loon. To them, I'm just a crank, another Denim Ghoul, though I guess to think they have noted my existence at all is just more self-deception.

I've told parts of this story to the Shits, but only Dyl knows all of the details.

"Okay," he says now. "No cops. Yet."

"Cool," I say.

SEVEN

That afternoon I'm back at the Stop Pit with Dyl and Cutwolf when Hera comes in, starts taping up flyers near the door.

"Hera," I say, walk over.

"Heard from him yet?"

"No," I say. "But there have been developments."

"I'm sure."

"Do you want to hear them?"

"Not really. Thorazine is playing a last-minute show tonight. You should come. It's in this guy's loft."

"Which guy?"

"This guy Wallach knows. It's in the West Village."

"The what?"

"It seems mythical, I know, but it's a real place."

"That area confuses me, Hera. The grid just falls apart."

"You have a very small life, Jack."

"Thank you."

"For what?"

"For remembering my new name."

"Anyway, you guys are welcome to come. I'll put your names on the guest list."

———

The loft is on Bethune Street. Cutwolf, Dyl, and I get lost a few times on the walk over. It's cold and the snow is falling again. I'm layered up, as usual, and Dyl is wearing this long, silly zebra-print coat, one he maybe thinks is outlandish enough to convince us he should join the Shits. Cutwolf shivers in the thin red Marlboro windbreaker he claimed with proof of purchase of 185 packs of cigarettes. He's got a ball cap and a bandanna from Philip Morris, too, but deems it "conspicuous consumption" to wear all of the items at once. He also claims he won't spend a dime on warm duds.

"Winter can fuck itself."

The loft is in an old brick building, maybe a former sweatshop. The street door is open and we climb a flight of worn wooden stairs. A woman in a prairie dress and a gold-sparkle crash helmet sits sentry on a stool.

"We're on the list," I say.

"Okay."

"Aren't you going to check?"

"I believe you."

"Come on," Cutwolf says. "There's no list. It's just a bunch of rich assholes in a loft."

"I'm not rich," says the woman. "I'm from fucking Allentown."

"And look where you are," Cutwolf says. "In the hallway."

"I'm the booker."

"For this place?"

"I work all over."

"Why would you book a show for a fool like Wallach?"

"Cutwolf," I say, throw the booker an apologetic look, but she stares at him, perhaps intrigued.

Cutwolf sticks out his hand. I'm not certain, but this might be his first attempt at a handshake in some time. He's more of the curt-nod type.

"Craig," he says, because that was his name before the Shits and probably will be after.

"That's not what your friend called you," the booker says. "What was that name?"

"Cutwolf," Cutwolf says, and now he delivers his most undiluted death stare, his eyes wide, his pupils dull buttons of stone. It's a sign of affection. The booker meets his gaze and holds it.

"I like Cutwolf better," she says. "Is that your last name? Is it Jewish?"

"It can be. Nice helmet."

"Thanks. I have a fucked-up skull."

"Sorry to hear it."

"It got fucked up in a traffic jam."

"Oh."

"I mean a traffic accident. See? I fucked up my brain too."

"You don't look brain-damaged to me," Cutwolf says.

"Thanks. Do you stare at people like this all the time?"

"Like what?"

"I don't know. Like they just stomped your hamster to death?"

"Sorry. It's my face."

"Don't be sorry. It's interesting."

I nudge Dyl.

"Let's go in," I say.

The loft is spacious and dark. Gel lights fixed to the rafters shine down on a Roland amplifier connected to an extravagant rack of effects pedals. This rig sits beside a lone snare drum on a narrow platform. Dyl and I huddle around a bar set up on a credenza near the stage. Beer and booze and buckets of ice. Groups mill about in silhouette. Somebody taps my arm.

"Jonathan?"

Because her hair is now lime green and shorn in some sparse, asymmetrical mode that resembles the coif I once saw in a science museum's life-size re-creation of Australopithecus, it takes me a moment to recognize my ex-girlfriend.

"Vesna," I say.

"Jonathan."

"Jack."

"As in Jack Shit? Nice." I almost want to kiss her for being the first person to appreciate my nomenclatural gesture, and also because I still want to kiss her. Though she's not, it turns out, as good a kisser as Corrina. It's not a question of skill. It's more a matter of conviction. Her affection never felt directed at me so much as at somebody I might become.

"Thanks, Vesna," I say. "You always did get my humor."

"I'm not sure it's humor, exactly, but I know what you mean. How are you?"

I doubt she cares that deeply, but I suppose she means how am I handling the pain of her absence, as well as any discomfort derived from said absence's blunt elucidation of my romantic inadequacy. It sucks to lose your girlfriend, and it also sucks to know you lost her because you suck at having a girlfriend.

If I were a more evolved, honest person I'd tell her the truth, that though I've moved on in some ways, it still hurts to be deserted, and that I'm also anxious about a number of specific concerns, such as the dissolution of my band, the pointless nature of life without it, my chronic penury, and, most acutely, the double disappearance of my bass and my roommate.

Instead, I say, "I'm fine."

"I'm glad," she says. "I felt awful ending things the way I did. But I think maybe I did us both a favor."

"I'm sorry," I say.

"For what?"

"For the flake-outs. And the whiskey dick."

"I was often grateful for the whiskey dick."

"I'm an idiot."

"It's okay. You just need an idiot girlfriend."

"Maybe you're right," I say, and my mind, like a shiny bird, alights on a branch wreathed in green, sun-honeyed leaves. There perches another bird, whom I take for a symbolic Corrina-mind.

"Besides, after my mother met you that one time she said you were too fat for me."

"Oh."

"But I told her to back off. It's not like we were going to have kids."

"I guess not," I say.

"Or wait, do you actually want kids? You're only twenty-four."

"Not now. Maybe when I'm more established."

"As what?"

I'm about to answer, to explain that despite Vesna's oft-stated doubts, I still believe in the vision that the Shits, whatever their current or future configuration, will bring to the table of innovative and eccentric guitar-based noise rock, a field, or table, that doesn't support a lot of careers but one that maybe rewards a few diligent and talented practitioners with a modicum of financial stability—take Mr. Thurston Moore's venerable outfit Sonic Youth, for example—when a tall, skinny dude with magazine cheekbones and ringlets of ash-blond hair glides up.

"Hey there," he says, laces his fingers into Vesna's hand.

"Hey, baby. Ned, this is Jonathan."

"Jack," I say.

"Right," Vesna says. "Jack."

"Though I'm the Jonathan Vesna has probably mentioned."

"Did you ever mention a Jonathan, babe?" Ned says.

"I don't think I did."

"Sorry," Ned says, rests his chin on Vesna's shoulder. "Doesn't ring a bell."

"Ned's in a band too," Vesna says.

"I know," I say, nod to Ned. He's the drummer for Mongoose Civique, a band I officially despise for their polished songcraft and serious major-label interest, and possibly subconsciously admire for similar reasons. They are deft, quasi-heavy, hooky in that anti-hook manner, a sort of frat-house Nirvana, or maybe, given the shimmering innocence of their lyrics, which tend to exalt bubble-gum kisses and cold mountain starlight, more of a tree-house Nirvana, which is not the worst thing, or else is very much the worst thing. Ever since those Seattle boys broke the indie piggy bank open, all of the A&R douches from the big labels have been scouring the land for the next underground bonanza.

Mongoose Civique certainly have no qualms about selling out to a major, and they have the looks and vapid, radio-friendly guitar crunch for a proper payoff. Sometimes I wonder how the Shits would face the dotted-line dilemma, but the truth is we might not have to worry about it, and not just because we're the Shits. You can already sense this gold rush ebbing.

Only the real, unremunerated artists will remain.

Meanwhile, bands like Mongoose Civique will hurry to pledge their gifts to the dominant ideological apparatus. I mean, sure, maybe most of us do in the end, but it's plain heinous how the fact doesn't seem to gnaw at those guys at all. They are the kind of band Toad Molotov believes will be first against the basement wall of CB's once the revolutionary punk rock firing squad gets cracking (though it does seem decades behind schedule). Which reminds me, I do need to get to Toad's place soon and see if he's heard from the Earl. But I still want to catch some of Thorazine's set.

"Jack used to play with Hera in the Shits," Vesna tells Ned now.

"Still do," I say, mention Hera's promise to play the farewell gig at Artaud's next week.

Ned flashes a gentle, condescending smile.

"Oh, man, you're in the Shits? You guys are a riot. So funny."

There is a misconception in some quarters that we are some sort of joke or novelty act, when what we do merely underscores the fact that all of the other bands are jokes, and deeply unfunny ones at that.

"Thanks," I say.

"Let's get some drinks," Ned says to Vesna, guides her toward the bar.

Dyl walks over with Cutwolf and the booker in the helmet. Her name, I learn, is Crystal. We press closer to the stage and about two dozen people gather in around us, pale, young humanoids in thrift-store T-shirts emblazoned with the logos of defunct power trios and discontinued soft drinks. They chatter, chuckle, shout. Their glib exuberance ripples through the warm room. The loft lights dim and two figures take the stage.

"Yeah!" somebody says.

"Wallach!"

"'Freebird'!" some dolt shouts. There is always one. I'm not exactly the world's hugest Skynyrd aficionado, but here's a possibly bitter-tasting verity: "Freebird" is an infinitely better song than anything some postcollegiate wag in a Mello Yello ringer tee could ever hope to conjure.

The players take their positions. Hera stands with one stick and a drum brush. Wallach, a gawky kid with a goatee, plugs in a custom-made guitar of exquisitely ribbed mahogany, fiddles with his pedals—wah-wah, reverb, looper, pitch shifter, flanger, phaser, fuzz—all mounted on a plywood board at his feet. The Apollo astronauts had fewer knobs to master. I peer over at Cutwolf, catch him sneering at the fastidious array.

"Hi," Wallach says. "We're Thorazine."

"Wooh!"

"Yeah!"

"Thanks for coming out. Means a lot to us. Okay, let's see here. Guess we'll play some of our stuff now."

If Cutwolf is contemptuous of Wallach's lavish rig, it's banter like this that gets my dander up. This bid for community, laid-back authenticity. Where's the theater, the spectacle, the deadpan menace? Any schmuck can break the fourth wall. Try fucking building one. Try walking onstage and erecting an invisible barrier of terrifying splendor all the way up to God.

Still, my ire dissipates once the music starts. To make way for new rage.

Hera hits the snare with her drumstick, a stuttering beat, like a robot on low battery. Wallach plinks his strings, a strange, disjointed riff. We all know he's a prodigy, could play waterfalls of flawless scales if he wanted, so we're meant to be impressed by this spare, unpleasant ditty. It never builds or shifts, but stays locked in the same dinky circuit. Every once in a while Wallach leans into the mic and makes a little yipping noise, like an anxious lapdog, or incants in a low growl:

> *And father is in the basement*
> *sanding down his rape boat*

and mother is in the kitchen with her broken blender
and split-apart split-level dreams
Yip! Yip!

All I can think is: Hera deserted the Shits for this? Hera, who hits like a thunder goddess in perfect 4/4 and can also put a round funky hitch in her beat, has forsaken the joys of our frenzied attack for this anemic bluster?

Now I know what that *Newsweek* in the Pinsk meant by the end of history.

"Fuck this," Cutwolf mutters, and we both turn away from the stage at the same time, make for the door. Dyl and Crystal catch up with us at the landing.

"Maybe it gets better," Dyl says. "They have some decent ideas. Sanding down a rape boat is a provocative image."

"Yip yip," Cutwolf says.

"I think that feedback is good for my brain," Crystal says. "I'm going back."

She grins at Cutwolf, plunges back into the dark of the loft.

"She likes you," I say.

Cutwolf spits on the floor.

"I think I saw Glenn Branca in there," Dyl says.

"Look," I say. "I don't have anything against them. They might even be good. I can't tell because my judgment is clouded by the fact that I'm pissed off at Hera."

"And because Wallach is a walking ball of smegma."

"You don't know him, Cut."

"I can hear him. Just play one real fucking chord, man!"

Some kids at the crowd's edge glare. Cutwolf returns optical fire. I proffer a palm of peace.

"Let's go see Toad," I say.

EIGHT

Near Toad's, a bundle of scarves and sweatshirts ambles toward us.

It's Our Lady of the Sealed Works. She knows the laws of layering too. She nods to me again, and this time I stop.

"Hey," I say.

Our Lady gazes up at me with clear, gentle eyes.

"You know me, right?" I say. "And do you remember the guy I'm always with?"

She shrugs.

"Good-looking guy?"

Our Lady grins.

"Have you seen him?"

Now Our Lady lifts her poncho, shows me her fanny pack, unzips it. She fingers the syringes in their plastic sleeves.

"Two dollars," she says.

"No," I say. "Have you seen the Earl? Tonight?"

"Give her the money," Cutwolf says. "Maybe she'll talk."

"Maybe I'll talk," she says.

"Here," Dyl says, digs in his ridiculous coat, tugs out two mashed-up dollar bills. I snatch the money and hand it to Our Lady. She slips a sealed syringe into my palm.

"No," I say. "I just need some information."

Our Lady smiles again, brushes past me, waddles away.

I stuff the works into my shirt pocket. Cutwolf curses the winter on one side of me, while Dyl yammers on about Glenn Branca's legendary symphony for a hundred electric guitars on the other.

"Come on, let's move it," I say.

Why must it always be me who remembers the mission?

A block from Toad's, Dyl peels off, says he needs to walk his dog. Cutwolf and I press on, ring Toad's buzzer. We wait for a while, ring it again. Cutwolf lights another Marlboro, maybe smoking his way to a ski jacket, or neoprene chaps.

"That girl with the helmet," he says.

"Yeah."

"Couldn't really tell if she was shittin' me about the brain damage."

"Who knows?"

"I mean, I guess we're all brain-damaged. By society."

"Good point."

Cutwolf sucks down the rest of his cigarette and tosses it like a dart, cherry first, at a parked car. It plops into a thin coat of snow on the hood. I remember the day I told Toad I was leaving TAOTSL to start the Shits with the Earl. We sat in his kitchen with a loaf of Wonder bread and a jar of mint jelly. Toad flicked a lit butt past my ear.

"You're going to leave me in the lurch," he said, "to go diddle around in some sellout artsy-fartsy dumb-fuck combo?"

I always find it amusing how we, the Shits, constantly complain about other bands being sellouts, but guys like Toad think the same about us. Somewhere, hunkered down near the godhead of bitterness, there's a dude in the rattiest cutoffs ever who must think the same about Toad. It's like Russian nesting dolls of impotent rage and insecurity. I'm just honored to be included.

"Sorry, Toad," I said that day in his kitchen.

Now I look up at his window, see shadows move behind the drawn shade.

"Toad!" I shout.

Cutwolf jams the buzzer again. He lights another cigarette, keeps his thumb on the button. We can hear it down here, faintly, on the snow-tamped street. Winter's amplifier. We wait another minute or two.

"Play the board," I say.

Cutwolf hits all the bells and soon the street door clicks.

Toad lives on the fifth floor and the stairs take us a while. We are young, but not specimens of rude health, what with my extra pounds and Cutwolf's Philip Morris–sponsored pulmonary system. But we do arrive in time to hear, from the other side of the door, a weird scuffling noise, followed by low moans.

"Toad?" I say. "Toad?"

The scuffling and moans get louder.

"Toad!"

"I'm gonna bust it down," Cutwolf says.

"Wait."

But Cutwolf is not big on waiting, and before I know what's happened, he's hurled himself against the door. He bounces off, clutches his shoulder.

"Nearly had it," he says.

The knob turns easily.

Toad's apartment is dark and rank and stinks of tequila. Shards of bottle glass, which we kick across the wet floor, glint in the moonlight that comes through the kitchen window. More noise erupts from behind Toad's bedroom door. I feel a hand on the back of my neck, choke down a scream.

"Shhh," Cutwolf says, pinches my shoulder. The sound of a

rattling window in the next room is followed by a metal clang. Cutwolf grabs a cast-iron pan off the stove, lifts it up like a war club. It's hot in this building, too; under my thermals, sweat trickles into my ass crack. Cutwolf taps my arm, points to the bedroom door. I throw it open.

Even as I flick on the light I see movement through the window. There's an immense, shadowed form on the fire escape, something long and rectangular in its grip. The sliding ladder rumbles and the dark shape dips out of view. We hear the sound of boots push off in the slush.

"No!" Cutwolf says, and I turn.

Toad lies sprawled on the worn plank floor. His legs, stiff and hairy, stick out from his shorts. The side of his face is mashed, dented. He's wearing a familiar T-shirt, the one that reads "The Annihilation of the Soft Left Is Hard for Revolt!" Blood burbles from a deep gouge in the "Soft," right over his heart.

Toad looks pretty dead, but when I lean down I hear moist, fluttery breaths, some last wedge of living lung, tiny, isolate, sawing away.

"Is he still alive?" Cutwolf says.

"Almost," I say.

NINE

Toad dies before the ambulance comes.

"There's nothing you could have done," the paramedic says, after inspecting the body.

"Unless you know basic CPR," his partner adds. "That might have helped."

Cutwolf and I stare down at the linoleum in shame, wait for the police to arrive.

This is a crime scene, the paramedics remind us. We'd better not touch a thing.

I haven't been around a lot of dead people before. Grandpa Abe died when I was eleven. I only ever knew him as an old gent with a rueful smile and a weak heart and then he was all waxy in a casket.

One night in college, after a daylong bong binge in which the hidden meaning (since forgotten) of the seven-year character arc of Detective Lieutenant Martin Castillo of the Metro-Dade Police Department's Organized Crime Bureau, Vice Division, had been revealed to me in a cathode-washed Damascene flash, I stepped out for some air, heard a voice shout, "Daddy!" from across the street.

In a driveway, under gold-brown garage light, I found a young woman stooped over a middle-aged man spread out in the gravel. Sprinkled around him like burial totems were a stitched leather key-ring pouch, a cigar stub, and a video-cassette. The man's face had gone blue. A thin bubble wobbled on his lips.

"Can you help him?" the woman shrieked.

"I don't think so," I said, looked down at the title of the videocassette. The irony of the man having just rented the Warren Beatty afterlife comedy *Heaven Can Wait* grew less delicious with each passing nanosecond.

Grandpa Abe and the blue man have drifted into abstraction, though they live rich, dormant lives as half-repressed traumas that continue to leap out at me in violent clatters.

We all have our snakes in a can. We all are the can.

But tonight, Toad's death is a hard chop to the gut, to the *kishkas*, as Grandpa Abe might have put it. My legs shake. I want to puke. I puke on my tongue. Who would do such a thing? He did not deserve this. He was another human like the rest of us, groping around in the dark in his pineapple juice–stained shorts. Now I'll never hear that reedy, hectoring voice again. Toad Molotov had his flaws, but he cared about this world, yearned in bad song to make it better.

When the detective arrives, he leads us back into the bedroom one at a time. Cutwolf goes first and I wait with the paramedics and a uniformed cop. Cutwolf comes out after about twenty minutes, gives me a look I can't quite read. The detective waves me into the bedroom.

I recognize the torn twin mattress that takes up most of the cramped room. I'd helped Toad haul it up here after his old one got crawly with bedbugs. A few books and magazines are stacked on a low shelf, including the *The Marx-Engels Reader* and an issue of *East Coast Rocker*. The detective shuts the door.

"Sorry, buddy," he says. "You guys were close?"

"We used to play music together."

"Cool."

The way he says the word startles me. He's young, a white dude, maybe just a few years older than me. He's got longish hair and this striped, hooded hippie shirt. Lose the detective's shield that dangles from his neck and he could be headed out to catch the Spin Doctors at Kenny's Castaways. I wonder if it's just a weird confluence, the fact that he's a cop who also dresses like a jam band fan, or if it's some kind of cover. Or maybe that's the point. Maybe the only hippies left are cops.

"So, your friend out there . . ."

"Yeah."

"He says the door was open and you guys just walked in."

"That's right."

"And you heard a noise? Saw something?"

I tell the cop about the noises, the burst, the thump and clang, the figure on the fire escape.

"And did you notice anything in particular about the, ah, figure, as you call it, on Mr. Molotov's fire escape?"

Despite everything, I have to smile at the words *Mr. Molotov*.

"What's funny?"

"Nothing," I say. "I guess I just never thought of him as Mr. Molotov. He would have found that strange."

"But that was his name."

"That was his rock name. Toad Molotov. I guess I never knew his real name."

"Howard Molotov. It's in the records."

"Howard Molotov?" I say. "No shit."

"What about my question? The fire escape?"

"He looked big."

"He? You sure?"

71

"No, I guess not. Just big. Very big."

"Did Mr. Molotov have any enemies that you know of?"

I try not to grin again.

"So that's a yes?"

"Toad is—was—a legend. Everybody knew him. Tons of people played with him. He could be really harsh. But he was on the side of good, you know?"

"Aren't we all," the cop says. "Look, I'm just trying to get a picture. It's late and I'm sure you and your friend are in shock. We'll be in touch if we need to. And if you think of anything else, let us know."

The cop hands me his card: DETECTIVE SHAD FIELDEN.

I open my shirt pocket to slip the card in and notice Fielden's eyes narrow. I peek down, see the sealed syringe poking up.

"Turn against the wall, asshole."

Fielden begins to frisk me, stops.

"You got anything else that could stick me?"

"No."

"Better not be lying."

"It's not mine."

"Possession is possession."

"Yeah, but is it nine-tenths of the law?"

"Don't be a wiseass."

Fielden pats me down until he's satisfied.

"You don't seem like a human pincushion. Just getting started?"

"It's not my thing."

"Whatever. Get the fuck out of here."

We step back into the kitchen and an older, dark-skinned guy wearing a baggy suit and a colorful tie greets us. He stands at the edge of the room, chews a candy bar.

"What's up, Juan?" Fielden says.

"They're sending over somebody to dust," Juan says.

"Get lost," Fielden says to me.

The paramedics have hoisted Toad's body to a gurney, pulled a sheet over his head. Specks of blood soak through.

I peer over at Cutwolf, nod.

We trudge out of Toad's place together. As we go, I notice something on the floor, wedged in under the fridge. It's my Rat. My distortion pedal. The side with my initials painted in white correction fluid sticks out. I want to pick it up, but something tells me to just keep walking.

Outside the snow has stopped. The air feels fragile, brittle, like you could break off a piece of it, peer through it like a frigid prism at this murderous world.

We watch the paramedics march out to the street with the gurney, slide the last original member of the Annihilation of the Soft Left into their ambulance.

The cops, the paramedics, they probably think it's the usual story. Some junkie standoff, or alkie scumbag drama, a fight over a few bucks, pointless, desperate, another nobody bleeding out.

And in their cruel way, they are partly right. But also, fuck them. We, or maybe just I, know some other things. There's my Rat, for instance. And what maybe resembled a guitar case in the hand of whoever climbed out of Toad's window. That means my bass was probably there. Which means what? I'm not sure yet, but it must have something to do with the Earl. And maybe that giant freak with the battle knife, Mounce. Was that him on the fire escape?

I glance up there now, follow the zag of iron stairs to the ladder that hangs just above the sidewalk.

Yesterday was years ago. So was this morning, when I just

figured this all for a simple theft motivated by pharmaceutical cravings. The Case of the Missing Bass. Maybe it even started that way. But it's something else now. I need to figure this out, and I'm not sure I want to talk it through with Cutwolf yet. Reason flees him sometimes.

The ambulance rumbles off.

"Goodbye, Toad," I say.

"I need a drink," Cutwolf says. "Pit?"

I look down at the smudged ink on my palm, the barely legible address written there.

"I'll catch you later," I say.

TEN

Corrina's place is a few blocks southeast of the Stop Pit, a one bedroom on Eldridge. The main room is painted a pretty custard color and scattered with art books and sketch pads and photography equipment. A huge pair of motorcycle boots sits near the door.

We settle on the sofa and sip tea, Red Zinger, which reminds me of my childhood in New Jersey, our family cupboard packed with all the Celestial Seasonings classics, Sleepytime, peppermint, Morning Thunder. It's best not to get too Prousty right now, and I'd rather not fall for a woman just because her herbal tea collection makes me feel temporarily defended from the predations of a brutal universe, but after what's happened, it's nice to just sit here and imbibe something innocuous. I'm glad I didn't go to the Stop Pit with Cutwolf. Still, I can't help but stare at the boots.

"Those look a little big for you," I say.

"They are. I've tried them. They're not mine. They're Mateo's."

Corrina lets the name hover in the air between us and I glimpse something delighted and demonic in her eyes, as though she's decided I might qualify as a suitable emotional chew toy. She's not wearing her nurse dress tonight. Instead, she's got on what I take to be her home wear: an old-lady smock, blue with yellow flowers; fishnet stockings; fuzzy slippers.

"Mateo?" I say.

"Mateo shares the rent with me."

"Oh."

"He's in Spain right now."

"Barcelona?"

"Madrid."

"Oh," I say. "Because I'm probably going to Barcelona soon. We'll be playing over there."

"That's so cool."

"I guess it is."

"Are you playing other places in Europe?"

"Not sure yet. There's a guy there putting it together. We have a pretty huge following in Catalonia."

"Well, if you go to Madrid, maybe Mateo can show you guys around."

"Maybe. Probably be tight with the schedule and all. Lots of shows and press stuff."

"When do you go?"

"Not sure yet."

We sit for another moment and I flash again on Toad's bashed-in face and punctured heart. Everything feels so confusing and horrible and there is nobody to talk to about it because Hera is onto her next life and Cutwolf's name might as well be Cutoff, at least when it comes to emotions, and Dyl is, well, Dyl, and here I am with this warm, sweet, and also possibly sadistic woman who maybe has a boyfriend and I've already lied to her about some nonexistent European rock tour. Sobs buck up and I can't cram them down. I bawl, spill hot Zinger on my jeans.

"Shit!"

Corrina fetches a rag, but the tea is already soaked in, like I've pissed myself. I'm moving into the sartorial terroir of the Denim Ghoul. After a while, I stop weeping, just sort of sniffle. Corrina nestles in beside me, slides an arm across my shoulder.

"What's wrong? Are you nervous about the tour?"

"There's no fucking tour," I say.

"What?"

I tell her everything about the Earl, the bass, Toad's murder.

"I'm so sorry," she says.

"Thanks."

"How can I help?"

"Just sitting with me is helping."

Here is where we just sit for a while, and also where after just sitting we lean into each other for the tender consolations of soft, animal nuzzles. The kiss, when it occurs, is almost like coming back after you've paused the VCR to get a snack but then forgot you were watching a movie, maybe some flick from the 1940s, full of private dicks and hoods with heaters, dark alleys and damaged lovers, drifters, horseplayers, molls. You've wandered off with your toast or saucer of sliced banana, flipped through some books, called a friend, which is just to say the kiss picks up right in the middle of that last one at the bathroom door of the Stop Pit so many hours ago. Our hands want in on the action, too, jut around under our clothes.

"How many layers do you have on?" Corrina says.

I peel off all my shirts and sweaters. Corrina's lips glide across my slack young chest. She climbs me, nudges her crotch up to my mouth.

"Hey, look," Corrina whispers. "My vagina wants to make out with you."

I huff heady tang through her fishnets, feel the blood rush to my roused regions, all my phallogocentrism sluicing down into the stiffening referent.

"Make out with my vagina, Jack Shit!" Corrina exhorts, and with whatever knowledge of such procedures I've acquired in my short life, I do.

ELEVEN

Later, we go get a drink at the Jew-Hater's bar.

The merry old pogromist, with his lovely shock of alabaster hair and craggy fascist visage, pours us free shots with our beers. Maybe he means to lubricate his audience.

"The Yids, they cut the penis," he says, casual, as though relaying news of an off-season baseball trade.

Corrina squints at him.

"You mean circumcision?"

"God makes people perfect. The penis, perfect. Why cut it up? Only the Yid thinks of that."

"Why would you take perfect God-made people," I say, "and beat them and shoot them into ditches?"

"Politics is complicated," the bartender says. "Look what this country did to the Indians."

"Two wrongs don't make a right," I say.

"Only a fucking American says that. I thought you were a Yid."

"I'm an American Jew."

"I forgive you."

"Fuck your forgiveness."

"Ha! Good one!"

"Did you kill civilians in the war?" Corrina asks.

"What a question. From such a pretty girl. No, of course not. That's my brother Gleb. Rest in peace."

"Isn't that your name, too?"

"Sure."

"Was that common back then?"

"Was what common?" Gleb says, moves off with his bar rag, turns up the TV.

"You don't really think there was a brother, do you?" says a guy at the end of the bar, an older Black dude with a remarkably spiky magenta Mohawk. It's Vincent Monroe, an old punk legend in the neighborhood who played guitar in the Fleshwounds back in the early '80s. Toad introduced us a while back, but I doubt he remembers me. I wouldn't mind talking to somebody who knew Toad, though I'm still feeling pretty shaky, keep seeing that bloody gouge in my old bandmate's chest.

"Vincent," I say.

"Do I know you?" he says, tugs at the collar of his studded leather jacket.

"Through Toad Molotov," I say.

"Howie?"

"Yeah."

"Oh."

"We hung out once a few years ago. Talked about the secret Black history of punk music."

"Big surprise."

"You told me about Pure Hell," I say, "and that band from Detroit. Death. How they were like the Black MC5."

"I bet I didn't say it like *that*."

"Maybe not. We also talked about that Lester Bangs essay where he writes about racism in punk and the stuff Ivan Julian in the Voidoids had to deal with."

"I know Ivan."

"You said that last time."

"Well, I guess when you're the Black guy with the Mohawk and the historical knowledge, you end up having the same conversation with a lot of people."

"You said that too," I say.

"You're pretty annoying, you know that?"

"And you also said that."

"God, Jack," Corrina says, laughs. "You really kind of *are*."

"Sorry," I say. "I hope you know it comes from deep respect."

"What, the pestering?"

"Yes. I want to know about my lineage."

"Trust me, we don't have the same lineage."

"I didn't mean it like that."

"I know how you meant it."

"Oh."

"So," Vincent says, swirls his drink. "How's old Howie doing?"

"He's dead," Corrina says.

I shoot her a look and she shrugs.

"Dead?" Vincent says. The news seems to knock him back. He steadies himself on his stool, grips the bar with silver-ringed fingers.

"Yeah," I say.

"Fuck. When?"

"About three hours ago," I say. "I was there, sort of."

Vincent slumps a little.

"That's really sad, man. What happened?"

"I don't know."

"I thought you said you were there."

"Sort of. Almost."

81

"The liver, right? Fuck."

"It wasn't like that. I mean, somebody did it to him."

"Like . . . killed him?"

"Yeah."

"That's fucking horrible, man. Who would do that to Howie?"

"I don't know," I say. "But I'm working on some theories."

"Howie," Vincent says, shakes his head, stares down at his hands. "Fucking Howie."

"I'm sorry," Corrina says.

"Honestly," Vincent says. "We weren't close or anything. I mean, Howie was an asshole. But, like, an honest asshole, you know? Least racist of all you motherfuckers too."

"He was a good man," I say.

"No, he wasn't. I just told you, he was an asshole."

"Right."

"Man, fuck, whoever killed him. I hope . . ."

Vincent bangs his fist on the bar.

"Me too," I say.

"What's your name again?" Vincent says.

"Jon—Jack Shit."

"Jon-Jack?"

"No. Just Jack. Jack Shit."

"He's in the Shits," Corrina says. "They're a band. You would like them."

"Oh yeah? You their publicist?"

"No," she says. "Just a friend."

Vincent nods, sips his whiskey.

"Every band needs friends," he says.

TWELVE

I walk Corrina home. She asks me up, but I tell her it's better if I'm alone.

"Are you sure?"

"Yeah."

"If it gets weird, just come over. I'll be up. I'm working on this video piece."

"Okay."

"Actually, I was going to ask you to be in it, but it's obviously not the right time."

"What do you want me to do in the video?"

"Well, the idea is you'd be naked, drenched in menstrual blood, and you'd do this kind of Jack Tripper *Three's Company* move, where you come in through a doorway, do a double take, drop to your knees, and scurry back out. Then there will be some quotes from Hildegard of Bingen transposed on the screen."

"I can do that," I say. "Especially now that I'm also named Jack."

"I'd really appreciate it."

"Who is Hildegard of Bingen?"

"She was a medieval nun. A mystic and a scientist."

"You can be both?" I say.

"In the Middle Ages you can. And someday soon, I hope."

"I promise that when I get a minute I will be happy to be your naked, blood-drenched John Ritter impersonator."

"Thanks."

"What are you going to use for menstrual blood?"

"Menstrual blood," Corrina says.

"Good idea."

"Authenticity's important. Though I have to mix it with other stuff. Otherwise it dries up."

"Smart."

We kiss for a while on Corrina's stoop. It's nearly 4 a.m.

Back in the Rock Rook I find a half-full forty of St. Ides in the fridge and take it into the Earl's sarcophagus, stretch out on his futon. He's got a little reading lamp clipped to a stool, a wooden cigar box with a painting of John Wayne on the lid. The Duke crouches, Colt Peacemaker in his hand. The Earl keeps his needles, spoons, and cotton in this box. A private joke between him and his habit, I guess, or between self-styled aristocrats, and a nod to that old '50s ditty "Duke of Earl."

Next to the box is the Earl's copy of Tosches's Hall & Oates biography. I flip it open to an underlined passage: "As often as not, Daryl's darkest and most misanthropic reflections were the reactions of a simmering rage born of romanticism . . . as only someone who still believed in, who wanted to believe in, the potential for human goodness (and there is really no other way to express that phrase, that notion, be one a double-knit preacher or a deluded French semiotician, a simpleton or a genius, a Faust or a Lou Costello)."

I take some umbrage at the line about the semiotician. What's Tosches's beef? He's an important critic, I know, but here he sounds like that fogey professor with the best-selling screed about today's postmodern college kids. I hope this doesn't represent the closing of Nick Tosches's mind. We are counting on discerning types like him to appreciate the aesthetic nuances of the Shits. The Earl and I have had long conversations about whether Tosches really admires Hall & Oates or not, and whether *Dangerous Dances* was a labor of love or some kind of make-a-buck quickie, or maybe both. I can't quite remember where we left it.

Here on his futon, I feel sad about the Earl all over again.

How could I, his friend, his bandmate, his sonic brother, let him slip so hard into the grips of bag fever?

What the hell were we thinking, all of us kids who moved to New York years too late, wearing the superannuated styles, doing the old, dirty drugs, coaxing the classic roar from our tube amps? In other precincts of the city, young people dance and heave to a modern throb in a whirl of rum-and-cokes and coke. Uptown, and in the boroughs, new rap galaxies explode into being. But here we are, sad stragglers, knockoffs, ensorcelled by the wizened gods. What gives?

Sometimes I wonder about it, but then I remember the opening thirteen or fourteen seconds of "TV Eye" by the Stooges, first Iggy's ferocious, frogged call—"Loooooorrrrrrrd!"—followed by the advent of the three kings—Asheton, Asheton, and Alexander (*gwee*-tar, fish, tubs). They prance wicked and regal through the moist halls of my mind's ear, and I remember why we journeyed to this teeming isle to conjure a dead time, or maybe resurrect it.

The funny thing is, the old deities still walk the earth. Or even the pavement.

Last summer, Cutwolf and I strolled home from practice

on Avenue B, argued about the new intro to "Invention of the Shipwreck."

I hated the intro, though I had written it.

"It sounds like Whitesnake," I said.

"No, it sounds like Dead Boys. Crossed with Can."

"It sounds like crap."

We passed beneath the awning of the Christodora on Tenth Street and there he stood, James Newell Osterberg Jr. himself, taking in the night air.

We learned later that he lived there, so it made sense, but still.

Cutwolf and I both felt him watch and appraise us as we passed him, our jeans, our T-shirts, our boots, our battered guitar cases, our bodies.

I glanced over, caught his eyes, alert, sharp, full of gentle mockery, but also tender. His TV eyes. He didn't hate us, but he saw us for what we weren't, and maybe never would be: a band worthy of existing even momentarily beneath the same canopy as the man who lost his heart on the burning sands.

Cutwolf and I were shaken, but the encounter, if you can call it that, filled us both with a secret light. We chucked the new intro to "Invention of the Shipwreck."

What the fuck did it need an intro for?

THIRTEEN

I fall asleep on the Earl's futon and only minutes later, it seems,
I wake, or not quite wake, but arrive at some fresh form of
sentience. All my days have been wiped away and I stand
now, apparently, in the cargo hold of a dank, corroded steamship.

I'm not alone. Dozens of us ragged souls huddle here, packed
in among burlap sacks, oak barrels, pinewood crates, most of us
pallid, fevered, the men with parched beards and threadbare
suit coats, the women wrapped in soiled shawls, kerchiefs. Bony
children crouch at the shins of their mothers, bunch there like
pocked fruit. The hold stinks of brine, rust, sweat, shit. What is
the meaning of this dim, miasmic hell, this seaborne dungeon?
Did I fall through the wormhole in the Banished Earl's arm?

Have the last twenty-four hours been a hideous, but also, at
certain junctures, namely the interlude at Corrina's, distinctly
sensuous dream?

I stare out of a porthole rimmed with rusted rivets, spot an
immense brown lady astride a tiny island. Her copper robes
ripple. She wears a spiked crown, brandishes a torch.

"My beautiful French bitch," the man beside me says. He's
a skinny fellow with damp, viral eyes. He shivers in his tattered
mesh half-shirt.

"Pardon?" I say.

"Oh, yeah. She'll ream you good. It'll be like eighteen eighty-one all over again."

"Eighteen eighty-one?"

"Baruch Liptak!" he says. "Don't you remember?"

"I remember," I lie. "By the way, it's Jack now."

"Okay, Jack."

"Who are you?"

"I'm the sick man from Europe," the man says.

"Do you mean *of* Europe?"

"No, just from, brother."

"Lady Liberty!" a man at another porthole cries.

Sailors scuttle down into the hold with trays of pizza. The scent of melted mozzarella twists my famished guts. The swabbies wave hot, glistening slices topped with sausage and green peppers, make lewd offers. Some of the women and children and men follow them into the shadows.

"They burned your father's house," the Sick Man says. "They killed his milk cow. Beat your brother into a coma. Baruch, you don't remember?"

"Maybe."

"America!" an old wraith of a rabbi shouts. "We're coming to America!"

Grandmaster Flash's "White Lines" pours out of a boom box propped on a crate of Speyside whiskey.

"Lev Gutkind!" shouts the rabbi. "Turn that down!"

"Baruch," the Sick Man says to me.

"It's Jack," I say.

"Baruch. You are Baruch Liptak. A tanner from Kiev. Welcome to the new world, my friend! You will settle in the Bronx and from your modest workshop you will craft cheap leather handbags and purses. Your son will be a schoolteacher. And his son will be a lawyer. And his son . . . well, that *vantz*, who can say?"

The Sick Man laughs, bangs his fist on the iron hull of the ship.

"I don't remember you being on this passage," I say.

"I wasn't. I'm the greeting committee."

"You know, I had a creative writing teacher in college who said, 'Write a dream, lose a reader.'"

"You didn't go to college. You're a tanner from Kiev, you fucking *schmendrik*."

The Sick Man cackles again, keeps banging his fist.

It would make for a more seamless transition if the sounds of the Sick Man's fist smashing the hull merged with the knocks at my front door, but I can't control such effects from slumber.

I wake in silence in the sarcophagus, *Dangerous Dances* open on my chest. I step out to the kitchen, still a bit dazed from my steamship dream, peel back the plastic lid of the Bustelo can, set to work on an acid jet-wash of a morning cup.

That's when the door knocks finally come, sharp, rabbity.

"Jonathan Liptak. Open up. It's Detective Fielden."

Truth is, it wasn't that many months ago that I stood for hours at this door's peephole, gooned on the Ajax crystal, listened for the slap of tactical boots on the stairwell. I was trapped, paralyzed between fight and flight, convinced the police had me surrounded.

Now it actually *is* the cops. Cops for real. Which could be the title of our next seven-inch if there ever is another one, or a disc of any diameter grooved with the tumultuous stylings of the Shits.

I let Fielden in. We sit at the red Formica two-top the Earl and I found in an alley and wedged between the shower and the kitchen window.

"Nice place," Fielden says.

I shrug. My moka pot spits, gurgles.

"Coffee?"

"No," he says.

Today he wears a wide-collar shirt under a blue leather jacket, flared slacks, pointy shoes. Between this getup and the hippie gear, I wonder if he's got some kind of fetish for '70s cops, or what he thinks of Frank Serpico, that disaffected detective who blew the whistle on police corruption and tried to live a happening life in Greenwich Village. Al Pacino played him in the movie, and if I were the law, that's the look I'd work.

"So," he says, opens his notepad, not the butter-soft leather-sleeved type the sergeant at the precinct house had, but a little drugstore Mead. "I just wanted to go over some details from last night."

"Have you caught the case?"

"Excuse me?"

"Isn't that what you guys say? When you're first on the scene and become the de facto lead investigator. You catch the case, right?"

"'De facto'?"

"Yeah."

"You watch a lot of cop shows?"

"When I was a kid, I guess. You know, they film a lot of the shows in this neighborhood. They like to set the junkie scenes down here."

"Do you feel like those shows do justice to your lifestyle?"

"I told you," I say. "That wasn't my spike. I'm not on that

stuff. But I won't lie. I know people who partake. But you're a homicide detective. You wouldn't care about that."

"Actually, I do care. I hate that shit. It's a fucking scourge. But I'm here about the murder last night."

"Funny thing is," I say, "these friends of mine told me how sometimes they go out to score on the corner, but the dealers have been scared off by the cops protecting the film crews. And then all these fake dealers, these actors, take over. Kind of weird if you pull back on it a little, like the simulacrum is always already—"

"Listen, Jack. Don't be nervous."

"Who said I was nervous?"

"Nobody."

"So that was like an observation? Cop intuition?"

"Let's just talk about last night. Why don't you run through what you told me? From when you left Bethune Street with your friends to when we spoke at Mr. Molotov's apartment."

"First you tell me your top five Dead songs."

"I'm not really a music guy."

"It's more of a Serpico thing?"

"Pardon?"

"The hair. The clothes."

"My girlfriend dresses me. She likes music."

"What does she like?"

"I don't know. Oh, right, what are they called? Stone Temple something?"

"That's not okay."

"Look," Fielden says, "I think we're moving toward a place that won't be conducive or pleasant for either of us."

"Fine," I say, run through the details I gave him earlier.

"And that's it?"

"That's it."

I set my coffee down. This is usually that moment in the morning when I'm finally wired up with enough caffeine to plug my bass into the mini-amp and start the old slap and tickle, though it should be noted I only play what could technically be called slap bass in the privacy of my own home. But now I remember all over again that my Fender is missing. The feeling is like a smack in the jaw from a phantom limb.

"You okay?"

"Yeah, why?"

"I thought you mumbled something," Fielden says. "Anyway, I'm going to level with you. We found something at the crime scene."

"What's that?"

"It's some kind of pedal. For the electric guitar. That's what they tell me. Weirdly, it has your initials on it. You want to explain that?"

"I have no idea."

"I don't believe you."

"You say you found it where? I haven't seen that thing in a while. It got swiped from a show months ago."

I'm not sure what I'm saying, but it feels important to stall Fielden until I can figure some things out.

"Don't lie to me."

"I'm not."

"Lying makes it so I can't help you. When you lie to me all I can do is stand back and watch you fuck yourself to death in the ass."

Here is a new Detective Fielden.

"I don't think I understand the image."

"That's because you're a soft little child from the suburbs."

"Yeah?" I say. "Where are you from?"

"Bay Ridge. You got a problem with that?"

"No."

"So talk to me."

"I don't know anything," I say.

"I bet your buddy does."

"I know this game."

"Some game. A guy is dead."

He's right, but I still don't want to open up about the disappearance of the Earl and my bass and how Dyl Becker called me from King Snake. I'm not ready to trust this cop. He might just be looking for a collar, a quick way to close the case, and I'm the potential patsy right in front of him. But I've got to give him something.

"Maybe ask that big prick Mounce," I blurt.

Fielden's mouth gets tight.

"Heidegger Mounce?"

"I don't know his first name."

"Big man?"

"Yes, very. And a huge head."

"That's him. Why do you mention him now? You know him?"

"No, but like, I just saw him once. In the neighborhood. And this guy on the street said his name. Said he was a killer. You're looking for a killer."

I'm really flailing now.

"Can you be more specific?"

"I wish I could. Why, do you know him?"

"We've liked him for a few things over the years."

"How could you possibly like that guy?"

"No, that just means—"

"Oh, right, I get it. They say that on TV too."

"Well," Fielden says, "even if he's not a killer, which I'm pretty sure he is, he's definitely been known to bust people up pretty bad. He's worked for the mob, for the Colombians, for the developers."

"The developers?"

"Real estate guys."

"He's a real estate agent?"

"That'd be good." Fielden laughs. "Open house with Heidy Mounce. No, idiot, he's muscle. Does jobs for uptown types."

"Jobs?"

"Security. Heavy errands. Last time we were looking at him he was doing freelance gigs. For big-timers. The people who own the city. The Dursts, the Speyers, Trump, people like that. You know what I mean? So let's try again. How did you run across him?"

Now there's another knock on the door.

"Shad?" calls a voice.

"Yo, in here."

Fielden stands, steps toward the door.

"My partner."

Fielden lets in the older guy from last night. Today's necktie is blue, patterned with tiny Porky Pigs.

Cop humor.

"Juan, this is Jack. Jack, Detective Juan Tabbert."

"Jack Shit," I say.

"Mr. Shit." Tabbert nods. "So, Shad, we good here?"

"Almost. What's up?"

"Talked to the landlord at Molotov's building. And a friend of Mr. Shit's here. Craig . . ." Tabbert glances down at his own tiny notepad. The Mead paper company must have a block-buster account with the police department.

"Dunn," I say.

"Right. Craig Dunn."

"He goes by Cutwolf," I say.

"He did mention that," Tabbert says. "Say, what kind of music do you fellas play?"

"Well," I say, "the zine *Morass* described it as post-wave neo-noise art punk with a sincere approach to irony."

"No shit? You like Prince?"

"Sure. He's a genius."

"Is your music anything like that?"

"No. We're in a different tradition."

"You mean you aren't as talented."

"Hey, you're the one with the gun."

"What the fuck is that supposed to mean?" Tabbert says.

"Juan, let's go."

"What the hell is this kid talking about?"

"Nothing. You just hurt his feelings. Let's get moving."

Fielden nudges his partner toward the door.

"And I wouldn't mess with this one," Fielden says, points at me. "He knows Heidy Mounce."

"No lie?"

"I told you," I say. "I don't know him!"

"Your story doesn't make much sense," Fielden says. "That's okay, for now. But pretty soon it won't be okay. Do you understand?"

"I think so."

"Follow your dreams, Mr. Shit," Tabbert says.

FOURTEEN

It's nearly noon and I'm late for my shift at Tony's Green Thumb, the plant service where I've been doing freelance care and watering for the last year. Whenever other work dries up, like the phone surveys or dishwashing gigs, I catch some shifts with the Thumb. Tony grew up with my dad, and his father started the business. Now the oldest Tony is dead and his son, my dad's old friend, is stuck home with a nerve disorder. He's a good man and it's sad to see him in this state. It's fallen to the youngest Tony, Tony the Third, or Tony the Turd to his employees, or at least this particular employee, to run the operation. Tony only calls me for downtown jobs. Today we meet at a converted bank on Lafayette. The landlords rent out the cavernous marble lobby for galas. Advertising and media firms, maybe working a boho angle, occupy the suites. Some of these companies really go in big for the foliage. Must be a morale booster to pretend your soul-macerating job happens in a hip forest.

"Where the fuck you been?" the Turd says as I walk into the lobby. "We got a bunch of snake plants and ZZs to unload."

The Turd is a short, chesty guy with a soft beaver face and sewer-rat eyes. He studied film in college and dreams of some-day being a movie reviewer on TV. He's even taped a photo of Gene Siskel to the dashboard of the Green Thumb van. Though his father's condition has forced him to put his aspirations on hold, he stays in practice, seeing several films a week and writing his reviews, which he sometimes distributes to clients when we happen to water their African violets.

Last week we did some fern work at a leading general interest magazine and the Turd casually slipped one of his critical forays under an editor's door. A corner peeked out and I snatched it up when he wasn't looking. It was a paean to Steven Segal's latest release:

> *The great Pauline Kael, who once answered one of my fan letters, said that if you are afraid of movies that excite your senses, then you are obviously just a jamoke. Or something like that. I am sure Steven Seagal, a brilliant actor who could break your face with a roundhouse kick at the drop of his ponytail due to his mastery of the venerable art of aikido, would also agree. Under Siege is as sharp and exciting a gift to the senses as I have experienced in some time, and I have seen movies by real so-called auteurs, including that prolific and, for my money, homosexual Kraut Fassbinder. But if Under Siege teaches us anything, it's that there is no shame in art that is about everyday red-blooded men reaching hard into themselves to find that aspect of them that's eager and able to defeat scumbags. From Homer to Chuck Norris, this has been a truism. We here at Tony's Green Thumb urge you to see Under Siege, and if you show us the ticket stub we will include a free pineapple sage plant with our service.*
>
> *Signed, Tony the Third*

Tony and I have not gotten along since we were kids forced to hang out during family visits. We'd play Showdown, a sort of Dungeons & Dragons set in the Old West, and Tony, who was always the saloonkeeper, this game's version of a dungeon master, cheated like crazy, which I'd call him on, to which he'd get indignant, and even take a swing. Some afternoons ended with us in a tangle on the carpet throwing punches until our dads burst in to break it up. They'd laugh at how "competitive" we both were, but later, still flush and shaky from the fight, I'd tell my father what had happened and he'd admit that even Mr. Opizzi, Tony the Turd's dad, could get hot under the collar sometimes, but that they were good people. I never did come around to finding the good in Tony, though I guess we tolerate each other for the sake of our fathers. I think he secretly hates me extra these days because he sees me following my dream while he has to run his father's business. I can't blame him for that. But he also doesn't hide contempt for the more out-there stuff that I favor. He knows zilch about music, for instance, besides whatever's on the classic rock block.

"Sorry, Tony," I say now. "It's been a rough twenty-four hours."

I start to tell him my woes, but he waves me off.

"Don't want to hear it, you degenerate. Just get the stuff out of the van."

"Sure thing, Tony," I say.

"I'm going to catch a matinee of *Unforgiven*."

"Okay," I say.

"Be my third time. A monumental film. And obviously Eastwood's swan song. The Western is the great American art form."

I wonder if he'd believed this when he used to rig the dice rolls in our Showdown games, leave my gunslinger slumped dead against a slop barrel behind the feed store.

"What about jazz?" I say. "I think that's probably the great American art form."

"The Western embodies our founding ideal of rugged individualism, and nobody is more rugged or individual than Clint. *Unforgiven* is a stern poem of death and regeneration."

"I saw it," I say. "Seemed pretty heavy on the death end."

"The blood nourishes the soil, you limousine liberal."

"I'm more of a hatchback Marxist," I say, but the Turd, as the Rolling Stones once put it, is on the run.

I carry the last of the plants and equipment inside and take everything up in the elevator, move through suites on several floors, watering, pruning, repotting. The people at their computers click away. Most are young, and maybe a few cruise the rock clubs at night, hunt for a song or a look or an attitude to appropriate for the marketing of sneakers, cars. Toad Molotov would be dousing the entire room in gasoline about now. I sprinkle a dwarf palm with nutrient-fortified distilled water. Better a living Shit than a dead Toad.

When I head back outside a few hours later, Tony is leaning up against the van.

"How was *Unforigven*?" I say.

"I saw *Lorenzo's Oil* instead."

"How was that?"

"Refreshing. A palate cleanser. You finish the job up there?"

"Sure did."

"What've you got going tonight? Playing a concert or something?"

Much as he looks down on me, I sometimes sense the Turd envies my life, or his fantasy of it. His version probably involves dressing rooms and horny groupies and platters of quality deli meat.

I tell him about the show at Artaud's Garage next Saturday.

"Is it like chicks in dog collars, that sort of scene?"

I think of Cutwolf's sister Drusilla, before she got hooked on fondant.

"Totally," I say. "Choke chains, latex, sexy girls with cat-o'-nine-tails."

"Rock 'n' roll." The Turd grins, slurps drool from his lip.

"All night," I say. "And party every day."

"Well, here you go," the Turd says, hands me the day's wages in cash.

I almost feel sorry for him, until I count my cut.

"It's short," I say. "You owe me another forty."

"Popcorn's expensive."

"Excuse me?"

"Listen, rock star," the Turd says, "even if I had two dicks and you sucked both of them, I still wouldn't give you a dime more. Find another job if you don't like it."

I won't win this war today.

"Asshole," I mutter.

I turn away from the Turd, head east.

Later I meet Cutwolf at the practice room. It's in the basement of an old building on the Bowery, one that I guess the developers Detective Fielden talked about haven't snatched up yet. We share the room and rent with a few other bands, including Vole and Lorna Prune. Kirby from the Prune said I could borrow his spare bass and his Boss distortion pedal, which he keeps in a closet here, if I was ever in a pinch. I hope this qualifies as a pinch.

It's Friday, our usual rehearsal night, but with the Earl missing and Hera too busy making more Thorazine flyers to join us, it's just Cut and me. We run through the set on guitar and bass, hammer out some changes. We still pray that the Earl will somehow materialize and Hera will keep her word about Artaud's and the original lineup of the Shits will have one last hurrah, or swan song, like Clint.

The prospect thrills me not just for the sake of a single appearance, but for how it will look from the vantage of time. I'm not imagining our show at Artaud's will have the broad cultural import of Dylan at Newport, or the Sex Pistols at the Manchester Free Trade Hall, or, speaking of farewell gigs, Lou Reed's last appearance with the Velvets at Max's Kansas City. It's too late in the day for that kind of status, but there's a chance the cognoscenti may eventually view our set at the Garage as a poignant and powerful hinge point in the history of underground music.

But we'd better bitch out hard, and we won't with Kirby's Peavey. It's too heavy, and the pickups are half-fried. It's okay for practice, but I'll have to head out to my parents' house in New Jersey tomorrow and retrieve my old Hondo from my bedroom closet. Can't say I'm crazy about the idea. My belly knots up just anticipating the psychic abuse that awaits back home, the family's feigned interest in my pursuits giving way to an amused condescension, which itself encrusts a sour, jellied center of profound disappointment. But I'll probably get a decent meal out of it.

Cutwolf and I blast through the bridge to "Orbit City Comedown."

"Just pause after the A minor," he says. "The Earl always does that wheezing thing right there."

We're about to start again when the door jiggles, swings open.

"Gentlemen."

"Hera," I say.

"Let me show you how the bridge works."

Fairfield County's fiercest scion slides in behind her Slingerlands.

"Shit," she says. "Left my snare at Wallach's."

"No problem," I say, lift the one from Vole's kit, carry it over. Hera gives it a few slaps with her hickory sticks.

"Out of tune," she says, takes out a drum key and tightens the skin.

I miss her precision, and watching her now kicks up memories of the Shits' early days, when we started to learn each other's quirks and gifts and curses. These moments are carved into me, like the first time I heard Cutwolf's guitar sound, those razory bursts he summoned with his twitchy strums, or saw how the Earl would transform onstage from a shy, funny drug fiend into this sun priest of a front man and from there to a sacred king, ready to be sacrificed for the unification of his people. It's all stitched into me, these memory strands. The threads shimmer, weave into a love story.

Weird to put it like that, but this band is my greatest love, at least so far, though maybe with the Shits nearly history, Corrina is the next part of the tale.

"Okay," Hera says. "Got it. Should we do 'Orbit'?"

"Let's try 'Horst' from the top instead," Cutwolf says.

Now we begin the slow-sludge stutter waltz of "Horst with No Name," play it all the way through without the vocals, build to the crazed finish. The cacophony sounds just right, or even goddamn glorious, the sadness of its passing built right into the peak. Like everything good, I guess.

FIFTEEN

We walk over to the Stop Pit after practice.

"I told Wallach about the show at Artaud's," Hera says on the way. "He's cool with it. He understands."

"How big of him."

"Cut," I say.

"Hera," says Cutwolf, "you know Wallach is a tool, right?"

"The right tool for the job."

"Jesus."

"I didn't mean it that way. Look, we are sleeping together, yes, but that's not the point. We are artists in a dialogue."

"But you play like shit with him," Cutwolf says.

"Cut," I say.

"She's my favorite drummer," Cutwolf says. "And he has her playing these stupid, pretentious beats."

"With Wallach it's more about the space," Hera says. "He wants me to play the space."

"I leave the space the fuck alone," Cutwolf says. "I let it be the space."

"Different approaches," I say.

"How's his rape boat?" Cutwolf says.

"His what?" Hera says.

We walk into the Pit, and Hod, Trancine's husband, nods to us.

"Hiya, young folk."

"Hey," I say.

Hod lines up our beers and shots. Hera lights a Kool. Cutwolf lights a Marlboro. I wave all the smoke away.

"Trancine says you all are looking for the kid that sings for you. The Polished Pearl?"

"The Banished Earl," I say.

"Right," Hod says, gives his muttonchop whiskers a pensive stroke. "You know, I saw him in here the other night."

"What?" I say.

"For real?" Cutwolf says.

"Yeah. He was sitting right over there. Didn't look too good. Little green around the gills. Kept nodding off. Had a bass with him."

"A Fender?"

"I don't know. He never took it out of the case. Just asked me if I wanted to buy a bass. I said no, I already have like four. And I never even played bass, not in the Saddle Sores or with anybody else. Always lead guitar. But stuff just collects around you, you know? What do I need four basses for? One's good for goofing around, maybe, or writing a song. But four? No, shit just gathers around you. Like the other day, I'm going through my closet and I find this mask. Like a wolf mask. Kind of corny, but also creepy, scary, you know? Either way, a pretty *specific* thing. You'd think I'd remember fucking *acquiring* it. But no. Never even knew I had it. Shit keeps drifting across the universe. We're just the dummies it sometimes catches on. You all see what I mean?"

"I do, man," Cutwolf says. "More than you know."

"Really?"

"Yeah."

"But Hod," Hera says. "Finish about Alan. The Earl. He asked you to buy the bass. Then what?"

"Then? I don't know. Or wait. Yeah. There was that guy."

"What guy?" I say.

"I don't know. Big motherfucker."

"Big?"

"Fucking head like one of those statues."

"Easter Island," I say.

"You know those boys were ancient astronauts, right?" Hod says. "That's how they had the technology to carve those giant heads."

"I think they were just clever," Hera says, landing a little British on the last word.

"What did the big guy do?" I say.

"Do?" Hod says. "I don't remember him doing anything. They were talking, him and your friend. And then they left together."

"They left together."

"Yeah."

"That's it?"

"Yeah, that's it. What, was I supposed to follow them?"

"You ever seen the guy before?" Cutwolf asks.

Hod draws his lips in a little. Something dark flickers in his eyes.

"Maybe. But I don't think so. I'd remember that head. But maybe I wouldn't. Like I said, it's just a lot of drift. Another round? On me."

Hod raps his knuckles on the bar, harder than when Trancine does it, flips his rag over his shoulder, moves off.

"Weird," Cutwolf says.

"That big guy he was talking about," I say. "Has to be the same guy who had my bass yesterday morning at King Snake. Has to be. I think it's this dude named Heidy Mounce."

"Heidi like the German girl?" Cutwolf says.

"No, short for Heidegger."

"Another German girl," Hera says.

"Have you even read Heidegger?" I say.

"I've read around him."

"What are we going to do?" Cutwolf says, shakes out the last cigarette from the pack into his mouth. He peels the top off the box, stuffs it in his pocket.

"Why don't you call that detective you spoke to?" Hera says.

"Fielden?" I say. "I don't know."

"Are we, like, suspects in Toad's murder?" Cutwolf says.

"Probably," I say. "I mean, they can't rule anything out."

"Maybe the sooner you tell this cop what we know," Hera says, "the sooner you'll be cleared."

"Maybe I will. I need to call Dyl, too, tell him to be careful. And I'll go to Jersey tomorrow. Get my Hondo."

Back in the Rock Rook, I try Dyl both at home and at the store, no answer. I spot Fielden's card on the kitchen table and call.

"Ninth Precinct, Detective DeGrasse speaking."

"Hello," I say. "I'm calling for Detective Fielden. Is he there?"

"Fielden? Hold on."

Now I can make out the detective's muffled voice over the line: "Anybody seen young Biff? No?"

"Hello?"

"Right," the detective says, back on the phone. "Sorry. Take a message?"

"Just tell him Jack Shit called. And that I know more about Mounce."

"Shit?"

"Or Liptak."

"Huh?"

"Either is fine."

"Jack Lipshitz has a tip on the Mouse? That's the message?"

"Sure, okay," I say. "I guess that works."

"Exciting stuff. You one of Fielden's frat brothers or something? This another prank? 'Cause I'm ready to break balls. Ask anybody about Cal DeGrasse. I'll come over there and hit your off switch. You understand?"

"Excuse me? No, this real."

But the phone is already dead.

I crack the forty of King Cobra I bought on the way home, settle into the Earl's sarcophagus. Something is wedged under the mattress, a paperback from the sidewalk canon, the Thomas Nashe book. I've never spent much time with *The Unfortunate Traveler, or the Life of Jack Wilton*, though I realize now my name change must have been partly, if subconsciously, influenced by the title. I leaf through the introduction by the poet John Berryman, that storied lush and eventual suicide, whose *Dream Songs* we used to read in college to justify, or at least adorn, our heavy drinking.

I find this passage: "All our lifetime the current has been setting towards licence. In Elizabeth's reign it was the opposite. Nothing seems to have been more saleable . . . than the censorious. We are overwhelmed by floods of morality from very young, very ignorant, and not very moral men. The glib harshness to us is a little repulsive. . . ."

I shut my eyes and try to picture the world of Thomas

Nashe, the horde of devious, grubby fellows in loose hose gorging on herring and ale. They conduct slanderous feuds via pamphlets, compete to utter the most felicitous and damning put-downs. What a clamorous, nasty place London must have been, where people flung calumny willy-nilly in dark barrooms and in hastily printed broadsides and everybody remarked upon your statements with near simultaneity. A cramped, cantankerous echo chamber where a few well-sunk reputational dirks left you bleeding out on the social sphere's tavern floor.

Here at the end of history, with the world so huge and diffuse, it's hard to imagine a realm so cruel and petty, or penned in.

Now an object grazes my face and I open my eyes. A photograph has fallen out of the book. I recognize the Earl's mother and father from the one time I met them, when they came to visit our apartment, so polite, horrified. They brought us a tray of Lebanese treats and the Earl's father fixed one of our cabinets. He's a successful contractor on Long Island. The Earl says he's done commercial work in New Jersey and Florida too.

I don't think the Earl's father understands anything about his son. Once, when the Earl's father nagged him over the phone about his refusal to pursue a viable trade, I wrote Mr. Massad a letter explaining the Earl's genius. I never heard back, except from the Earl, who was not exactly pleased after his father called him about it.

"What were you thinking, Jonathan?" he said. "He doesn't give a fuck about Baudelaire, or the Fall, or Vito Acconci, or early Television. He just wants me to find steady work."

I'm probably not at the top of Mr. Massad's list of people he'd like to hear from, but I know I should give him a call. Maybe he's heard from the Earl. Maybe the Earl caught a train home to Long Island.

I get the number from the operator. The Massads' machine picks up.

"Oh, hey," I say. "This is Jack—I mean Jonathan. Alan's roommate? I was just calling because . . . well, I was wondering if he's with you guys. Anyway, I'm sorry to bother you. Don't worry about returning my call. I'll call back if . . . well, I'm sure I'll hear from him soon. Thanks."

I do think Mr. Massad loves the Earl. You can see the kindness in the bright, black eyes of the man in the photograph. He stands with his wife, both of them handsome, beaming. Mr. Massad's muscled arms are folded over a polo shirt that bears the name of his firm: American Builders. The Earl's demons must hail from somewhere, but their origin is surely of an older provenance, perhaps not even terrestrial but something brought down by ancient star hoppers. The people in this photo appear too sweet, and perhaps too oblivious, to be the source. They do not resemble a couple with any intimation that their cherished boychild is a potentially world-historical punk rock provocateur, a jittery junkie, and maybe already dead.

SIXTEEN

The bus from Port Authority lets me off on Hawthorn Street, near the fountain downtown where we used to gather to smoke bones and drink beer and swap news of keggers and rumors of keggers in adjoining townships. Fresh party litter—crushed Busch cans, cigarette butts—suggests the practice has not abated since I left Merritt Heights.

I hike a half mile through snowbanks to my old house on Caldwell Lane. This is a town without sidewalks, without pedestrians, really, except for schoolkids and drunks on suspension, or people too old or confused to drive. The slush and snow soak my used Puma suedes.

I haven't been home much lately, and each time I come the house looks a little different, though not smaller. I just notice new things. A crack in the ice-slick flagstones. Ruffles of peeled paint on the shutter slats. But it's still the same pea-green split-level on the same drab cul-de-sac.

My mother greets me at the door, hustles me into the foyer. She's wearing my father's old fisherman's sweater. Her wavy black hair has new streaks of white.

"You must be chilled," she says. "Take off your sneakers and hang up your coat. I'll make you some tea."

"Barbara, is that him!" my father calls from the basement.

"It's him!"

"Be right up!"

"He's working on a big case right now. Big enough to keep him in the basement, anyway."

"How's school?" I say.

"It's okay. I have some talented kids this year."

My mother waves a variety pack of Celestial Seasonings.

"Peppermint okay?"

"Sure. Or do you have any Red Zinger?"

"Let me look."

"Corrina likes Red Zinger," I say.

Sometimes it's best to lay the life update offering on my mother's altar immediately.

"Corrina?"

"Yes."

"'Corinne Corrina'!" my mother belts, rolls her hips.

"Mom!"

"Big Joe Turner. Remember? I used to play it for you!"

"I remember."

"What's she like?"

"She's really nice. She's an artist. She's going to drench me with her menstrual blood."

"They're still doing that?"

My mother used to "make the scene," as she likes to put it. She was even in a group painting show and once attended a party where Andy Warhol was a guest, which she rarely lets us forget.

"Yeah," I say. "I guess they are."

"Well, I hope you're being safe about it," my mother says, drops our teabags into mugs, flicks a look at the kettle. "Did she get an AIDS test?"

"Of course," I say, though I have no idea.

111

"How long are you staying? You didn't say on the phone. Should I clean out your room? I've been drawing in there."

"Just the night. I came to pick up my bass."

"We're happy to have you for as long as you need."

"I know, Mom."

"Okay, honey. I was just making sure you knew."

"I know."

"No reason to get tense."

"Not tense," I say.

"He said through clenched teeth. Just clear off the bed when you want to sleep. I left a clean towel in there. Will you be joining us for dinner?"

"Sure."

"We're having guests. Aunt Helen and her new boyfriend."

"Oh, well, then maybe—"

"Please, Jonathan. I know Helen can be a bit much. But she's family."

"I guess we're all a bit much," I say.

"Thanks, sweetie. And maybe it will be interesting. Believe it or not, her boyfriend is apparently some kind of writer. Not really Helen's usual catch."

My mother serves Cornish hen and asparagus in the dining room. Outside the bay window, a crescent moon hangs above the county reservoir.

My mother's younger sister, Helen, has arrived in a lavender cashmere sweater and orange neckerchief, her black wavy hair, exactly like my mother's but without the white flecks, up in a twist. She's always been known as the "fun" aunt, which I guess is code for manic-depressive or something. Her date is not only a writer but one I've actually read. He was a cult figure in college, one of those novelists who might not be on the syllabus but about whom professors gushed in office hours.

His name is Guidry Tellman, but tonight he asks us to call him Bink.

How Helen, who usually consorts with local racquetball pros and blowhound accountants, ended up with the author of the prizewinning campus parable *The Unbeatable Slow Machine* as well as the postmodern sex-and-football satire *In Man Coverage*, just to name two titles I know, is beyond me, but I'm too mesmerized by Bink's presence—most notably his demonically lush eyebrow hair, his herringbone jacket, his silver and turquoise jewelry and pale, immaculately shaven head—to pay much heed to the story Helen unfurls about their first encounter.

Still, I doubt any detail is as salient as the fact that Helen, who deals in antique furniture, is a vivacious forty-year-old living on a respectable but glamor-crimping salary and Guidry Tellman, aka Bink, is not only an "active and interesting" (Helen's words to my mother) sixty-two-year-old man, but one of means, the owner of, my mother informs me before dinner, a duplex in Manhattan and a "cottage" upstate. I also recall that his book *Lumbago*, a rather experimental novel about a womanizing chiropractor forced to care for his crippled kid brother, a Vietnam vet, became an Oscar-winning film with Dustin Hoffman and Jan-Michael Vincent. He must have made some money, though who knows how box office profits work. I'd ask Tony about it, but I doubt he knows much about the inner workings of Hollywood, and also then I'd be talking to Tony.

I dice up my asparagus while my father launches into one of his rambling legal monologues about public utilities. He's a

lawyer for the state. Bink peppers him with some jurispruden-
tial arcana. Mark Liptak is impressed.

"You know your stuff."

"I attended NYU Law, back in antiquity."

"Never practiced?"

"Never finished. The siren call of prose fiction led me to my
current and long-standing distress."

"The arts can certainly be seductive," my mother says. "I
know from personal experience."

"Here we go," Helen says.

My father and I chew our chicken. Can you hear the anxious clinking of fork tines on semifine china? We wait for my
mother to make her move, but Bink wades right in.

"What kind of personal experience?"

"Well, let's just say I used to be in various artistic scenes
myself. And I was at a party with Warhol once."

"Really," Bink says.

"Mark was there too."

"Were those your wild days, Pops?" I say, throw him a not-
unaffectionate Dad's-a-dork smirk.

"It was a big party in the Village," my mother says. "Lots
of fabulous downtown types. Anyway, we have our fun and
now it's time to go home and we head to the elevator. It's one
of those big freight elevators, with the gate. And who is there
but Andy, with two of his Factory women. I mean, they were
dressed like women, but who knows? So beautiful and chic,
regardless. Mark, of course, has forgotten his coat. He has to
run back. The elevator opens and Andy and his friends get in.
And Andy looks right at me with that funny sphinxlike smile.
'I think you should come with us,' he says. It's as though he
doesn't just mean the elevator. It feels like he's inviting me into

a brand-new life. One I'd been dreaming about. But I tell him no. I have to wait for Mark. Andy just shakes his head sadly. The elevator door closes."

My mother reaches over and clasps my father's hand, smiles fondly at him. My father pushes at the hen bones on his plate. Maybe Bink expects a redemptive coda about how my mother, with the wisdom of hindsight, now sees she made the correct choice. The rest of us know better.

"So, Jonathan," Helen says. "How is your music career going? Do you have a record deal yet?"

"Working on it," I say. "We seem to have a following in Europe."

"That's wonderful!"

"Jimi Hendrix had to get famous in England first," my father says. "Sometimes it just goes that way."

"Yep," I say. "And the Ox Felchers live in Toledo but are actually more popular in Chapel Hill."

"Fancy that," my mother says, after some silence.

"It's true," I say.

I don't mention the buzz around our last seven-inch, which the zine *Soul Lobotomy* called "the most promising wedge of deconstructed neo-proto-art-scuzz since Gimp Mask Goethe's notorious debut."

"Jonathan," Bink says.

"Actually, I'm going by Jack now."

"Really?" Helen says.

"Honey," my mother says. "You're changing your name?"

"Well, you can still call me Jonathan."

"Jack Liptak," my father says. "It's got a nice ring to it."

"Jack Shit," I say.

"Oh dear," my mother says.

"So, Jack," Bink says. "You ever heard of a guy named Alan Vega?"

"From Suicide? Of course."

"Who committed suicide now, Bink?" my father asks. "A friend of yours?"

"No, Alan was in a band called Suicide. My brother was friends with him. Back in Brooklyn. He changed his name too. From Boruch Bermowitz. They were a little younger. About your dad's age."

"I knew he was really old," I say, recalling my argument with Cutwolf about the future of the Shits and feeling bad about calling Vega old, since he's younger than Bink, but the novelist appears unfazed.

"I saw them perform a few times in the seventies. Remarkable combination of poetic intensity and quasi-parodic abjection."

"You saw Suicide?"

"Vega swung a bike chain at the audience."

"That's amazing."

"Jonathan's group is called the Shits," my mother says. "So Jack Shit makes sense, I guess."

"It's not a group, Mom. We don't use that word."

"Honey, is everybody else called Shit too?"

"Just me, I guess."

"I'm sure Helen and I would love to come see you play," Bink says.

"Oh, absolutely," Helen says.

"They're loud," my mother says.

"Hendrix was loud," my father says.

"Jonathan played me a tape," my mother says. "You can't make out the words. But they have a good beat. They have this nice girl playing drums."

"Hera," I say.

"Tell me, Jonathan," my mother says, "do Hera and Corrina get along? Corrina is Jonathan's new girlfriend."

"Mom—"

"Just wondering."

"They haven't met."

"They haven't?"

"Good for you, kid," my father says. "Don't crap in your rice bowl. That's what I always say."

"What does crapping have to do with it?" my mother says. "Or rice?"

"It's a figure of speech, Barbara. I'm sure Andy Warhol knew all about it."

"I'm not so sure Andy crapped at all!" my mother says, laughs like she's maybe still at that famous party.

After dinner, while my mother and father wash dishes and bicker, Bink, Helen, and I sit in the living room with bowls of rocky road ice cream. Helen turns on the TV.

"Oh, I used to love this!"

It's an old rerun of a local late-night talk show. Helen tells us she always admired the host's sophistication and journalistic integrity.

"Admit it," Bink says. "You just have a crush on him."

"Oh, please," Helen says. "Though he is handsome. And isn't it funny how close his name is to mine? Or ours? His name is Lipsyte. Can you believe that, Jonathan? Robert Lipsyte. I bet we are related. It's probably just some Ellis Island mix-up that he's not Liptak. Though he doesn't really look like us. But that smile, that's kind of like Uncle Gil, right?"

"Jesus," Bink says.

"What's wrong?" Helen says.

"Nothing. Just look who the guest is. That fucking clown."

The host of the show grips his Lucite clipboard, holds forth with tough, slightly smug charm while his guest, a familiar-looking man in a power suit with a protruding lower lip and a sweep of blond hair, nods along.

"You may dismiss it," the host says, after mentioning the guest's out-of-pocket renovation of Central Park's Wollman ice-skating rink, "but people are talking about Donald Trump for president. What they're really talking about is: Donald Trump, show us the way."

"Please don't show me the fucking way," Bink says. "Helen, turn it off. Don't be fooled by this piece of shit, kid."

"Never really gave him much thought," I say.

"Well, you should. He's a symptom of the decay. The moral decay. The civic decay. The city's been bought up by bastards like this. Someday there will be no ordinary neighborhoods. Just the ultrarich and their urban serfs. Meantime we celebrate mobbed-up frauds like this guy. I know people who've worked with him. He's bullshit."

"Calm down, Bink," Helen says, but I'm kind of enjoying the novelist's diatribe. It reminds me of Toad at his most ornery.

"Just turn it off," Bink says.

"The host is actually challenging him," Helen says. "If you'd listen. Oh, forget it."

Helen clicks off the TV. Bink stands, paces the room, conducts some inner symphony with his ice cream spoon.

"Jonathan," he says. "Or Jack, rather. Jack Shit! Young people like you need to understand what's going on. Now, it's true this country is steeped in blood. Make no mistake about that. Ask the Chippewa. Ask the Apache. Ask the Gambian men on the auction blocks up and down the seaboard. We slaughtered and enslaved. I mean, you didn't. I didn't. Our ancestors were too busy mucking around in the shtetl or getting horsewhipped by Cossacks. But make no mistake, we've shared in the rewards reaped from these foundational atrocities. We can never forget that. Of course, all civilizations are soaked in blood. Egypt. Babylon. Athens. Rome. Tenochtitlán. Berlin. Moscow. It's never not been a gruesome, stabby death orgy. We're the shame of the great apes. And maybe it will always be so. But. And yet. We here in America, my friend. No, I won't say we are an exception. Of course not. But we might be an acceleration. In either direction. Toward total and irrevocable destruction of our world. Or maybe something else. Maybe something better. I know it sounds vague. It can only be vague at this point. But now there is this last chance that humanity can finally join together. Look, I'm a cynical old bastard from Flatbush. But it's easy to see what's coming down the pike. Do you know anything about greenhouse gases? Or food production? Population explosion? Are you aware of the ways transnational corporate consolidation creates entities more powerful and with greater reach into the lives of people around the world than anything seen on earth before? Genghis Khan? Alexander? Napoleon? Small-town mayors in comparison. The British Empire, by the end, was a stale, crumbling biscuit. It's been a good run for the Americans since World War Two, and maybe Slick Willie will keep things rolling for a while. But eventually the gravy train grinds to a halt. And when it does we'll be in some kind of high-tech feudalism. Life expectancy will go down. Real wages will stagnate. Of course, they already have. Thing is, we'll all be one giant underclass, but we'll be too busy driving our gas guzzlers to the video store to rent Bruce Willis movies to know it. Yippie-kiyay, motherfucker, is right. Yippie-kiyay to any dream of a shared human project on a planet that isn't going straight to hell. That isn't—"

"Bink?" Helen says.

Bink stops, lowers his spoon.

"What?"

"Maybe that's enough."

"I'm just thinking out loud, babe. Sorry."

"No," I say. "This is interesting. Have you seen *Under Siege?*"

"I haven't."

"Me neither."

"I know I shouldn't care about all of this stuff," Bink says. "By the time the shit really hits the fan, I will be living in a computer."

"You will?" I say. "How?"

"It's hard to explain. I'm not being coy. One of the guys who created Fortran has promised to assist me. Met him at a PEN thing. Do you know what Fortran is? The computer language? The point is, I'm going in. I will be programmed into a computer. My consciousness. Uplinked, or whatever. Like those cyberpunk fellows."

"What about me?" Helen says. "Do I get to come?"

Bink breathes out, grins.

"Sure. Why not."

"Will you be able to write your books inside the computer?" I say.

"Books? For fuck's sake, Jack. Write books? My God. Why? To do what? To show everybody how clever I am? Or how much I've suffered? Or how much I care about the suffering of others? It's all horseshit. Maybe it always was. It's not as though the real grown-ups, the people trying to solve the problems ever—I mean, did Dag Hammarskjöld read *The Recognitions*? I fucking doubt it. But none of this matters. Like I told you, I am going into the computer. Into the belly of the machine. And I will be a conscious agent. That's what the scientist who created Fortran, perhaps the greatest work of imaginative writing of the last thousand years, told me at the PEN open bar. I will be conscious. And you, my pulchritudinous Helen, if you wish to join me, you will be conscious too. We will shack up together in the motherboard. But we will not be writing any fucking books. Best-case scenario we will emit a sequence of gentle beeps. I will enjoy that. What do you think, Jack Shit? Care to join us inside the circuitry of a room-size computer? We can be an ersatz family, forever."

"No, thanks," I say. "I'm really just here to get my backup bass. We've got a show next week."

"Fair enough. I think I need another drink."

"Bink, sweetie. We should head back to the city soon."

Now my father barrels into the living room with a Scrabble box.

"Who's up for a game!"

Bink stares at him.

"Bink?"

"Beep," Bink says softly. "Beep. Beep."

My father wheels, heads back into the kitchen. Helen follows, calls out to her sister.

"Let me help, Barbara!"

"Oh, now you want to help!" I hear my mother shout. "When it's almost done. That's your oldest trick, Helly."

Bink levels a stern gaze.

"What's your objective opinion of this family?"

121

"Objective?" I say.

"Helen is a supple and open-minded lover."

"I'm not the right conversation partner for that particular topic."

"Understood. What happened to your regular bass? Why have you come for the backup?"

"Why do you care?"

"Details interest me. God, or the devil, depending on whom you talk to, resides in them."

"Our singer stole my bass. Or borrowed it. I don't know. He's disappeared. I'm looking for him."

"Are you worried?"

"Yes," I say.

"I know some fellows on the force," Bink says, lowers his long body onto the sofa, stretches, yawns. "They owe me."

"That's nice of you, but no, thanks."

"No idea where your friend is?"

"He's not in the usual places."

"Perhaps he's fallen among thieves. Lies by the roadside on his back. You need to help him."

"I'm trying."

"Brushing from whom the stiffened puke, I put him all into my arms, and staggered banged with terror through a million, billion, trillion stars."

"I like that."

"Edward Estlin Cummings."

"'e. e.' lowercase?"

"Correct."

"In college they said he was an anti-Semite."

"No question. But at least he wasn't Jewish. What's your excuse? Or mine?"

"Huh?"

"Think about it."

"Okay."

"Where I'm going, Jack, it's all ones and zeroes. It's the house of Yahweh. Ones are the bricks. Zeroes are the mortar. Can you dig that?"

"I think so."

"I'm glad. Beep-beep."

SEVENTEEN

After Bink and Helen leave, I go up to my room. I've already retrieved my Hondo from the closet. It's really a Fender Precision knockoff, black with a white pickguard. I'm fond of my Hondo. It's not the finest instrument in the world, but it's sturdy.

Here in my old room, the Hondo on my knee, I tingle with teen memories, the voluptuous agony. I recall the hours I'd stare at the water stain (it's still there) or pump away on my back like a living, wheezing, sperm-extracting derrick.

I also remember the times lost to the mirror on my door, a tennis racket, fastened by a robe belt—and later this very Hondo, hanging from a cheap strap—slung around my neck. I'd play along to the bass lines that thumped out of my plastic Kenwood stereo. A band is a body. The singer is the head, the guitars the guts and genitals, the drums the arms and legs. But the bass is the heart, the heartbeat.

What flows through them all, that's blood, the blood electrics.

My father is a decent man but he works too hard. He never understood how my indolence, my wallowing, was a kind of industry. My mother was more like me, so we fought forever. Life in this house was both incendiary and remote. It was just the three of us. But mostly I was alone in this room with the blue walls and the brown bedspread, dreaming of the day I could leave, join another body better than my own.

I found it for a while.

I pull the covers up and fall asleep trying to list every Shits show in chronological order, from those first appearances in somebody's basement to gigs at the Spiral, the Pyramid Club, even a mop-up spot at CB's. It's true we've never been the tightest band, but some nights we are the weirdest. When we are off, we are terrible. We don't have competent mediocrity to fall back on. And when we are on, we are still terrible but also one of the best bands you ever saw. That's how Dyl Becker put it, anyway.

Maybe that's why I dream about Dyl once I fall off into sleep. He stands astride a snowcapped mountain, rips a blistering and rather derivative guitar solo on a gold Les Paul. I notice that his patch cord is plugged into a socket in the rock face. There's a metal switch, a red light. The mountain *is* the amp! His solo rings out across the winter valley.

I wake up a little after dawn, the dream still fresh. It slides into thoughts of the Earl.

I should try to reach his parents again. They may have called me back with news. I tiptoe out to the hallway for the cordless phone, bring it back to my room, call the number I wrote down yesterday on a scrap of paper and stuffed in my jeans.

"Hello?" Mr. Massad answers in his kindly baritone. His voice is much less scratchy than his son's. I picture him on a wall phone in his kitchen like the one in my parents' house, blueprints rolled up in his hand, hard hat under his arm, almost out the door to some construction site.

"Hi, Mr. Massad. I called before? About your son? I'm his roommate."

"You called? I must have missed it. Which son?"

I've forgotten for a moment that the Earl has three brothers.

"Alan," I say. "Have you seen him, by any chance?"

"Alan?" Mr. Massad lets out a tight laugh. "No, I haven't seen him in a while. Wait, you're the one who wrote me that letter?"

"Yes, sir."

"And you haven't seen him?"

"Not for a few days."

"Well, is that unusual? I mean, I don't really know what you kids are up to, but sometimes I wonder. Level with me. Is my son on drugs?"

I remember now that Alan's oldest brother had a bad coke habit. I'm sure Mr. Massad hoped his other sons might avoid this sort of trouble. I guess it's better to come clean than keep covering for the Earl.

"I'm sorry, Mr. Massad. I've been encouraging him to knock it off. He seemed to be doing better. But I'm a little worried. He always comes home. He loves his sarcophagus. I mean, who wouldn't, and I don't know, after I heard Mounce say his name . . . but still, Detective Fielden doesn't seem to be doing much even though he said he'd look into it. And then Hod at the Stop Pit says he saw them together, though he didn't know the guy's name, but I mean it was obvious that—"

"Whoa, whoa, slow down."

"Sorry," I say. "Guess I'm worked up."

"Did you say Mounce?"

"Yeah, why?"

"As in Heidy Mounce?"

"Well, he didn't tell me his name, but yeah, I'm pretty sure that's it."

"Son of a gun," Mr. Massad says, and I recall the Earl once telling me his father never swears.

"You know him?"

"Yeah, I know him. He's a goon. I can't believe this. You say he was talking with Alan? It's a bridge too far, son, sending gorillas. That crook. Well, the heck with him. Can't scare me no matter who he sends. I stand my ground. I'm an honest man, son, and you know what? I have my rights. Who does he think he is, anyway? My family's been in this country longer than his."

"Wait, who?" I say. "Mounce?"

"No, not Mounce. Not even the one who probably sent him. I'm talking about the big boss. Did construction work on his hotel in Atlantic City and the man refused to pay me. For no reason. Just greed. So, I started to make a stink. Normally they just crush you with lawyers, but I found a smart one myself. Got that big blond idiot dead to rights. All he cares about is getting his picture in the paper. Never mind. We need to find Alan."

"I know. Look, I've been talking to a cop. He knows who Mounce is."

"What cop?"

"Shad Fielden. At the Ninth Precinct."

"He was looking for Alan?"

"No, he was checking into something else. Probably unrelated."

I decide not to mention Toad at the moment. It might worry Mr. Massad too much, and I've already spilled some beans I'd meant to keep on the shelf.

"A lot of city cops are in their pocket, son. But I'll look into it from here."

"Okay."

127

"Don't go poking around those people. Be careful."

"I will."

Mr. Massad hangs up.

I try to calm myself, pluck out the bass line to "Salad of the Bad Café," an early and long-discarded Shits anthem, watch the sun climb out over the gray, shingled rooftops of Merritt Heights.

My father makes me scrambled eggs for breakfast, nibbles on a bran muffin while I eat.

"I put onion in, the way you like."

"Thanks," I say. "So, how's the case going?"

"Making headway. A lot of moving parts. Speaking of headway, have you given any more thought to future endeavors?"

"Like what?"

"I don't know. Grad school. Or, God forbid, law school."

"I don't really see myself in a classroom right now."

"At your age I was just starting my professional life."

"The nineteen thirties were a different time."

"Funny."

"Look, Dad. I'll figure it out. I just have a lot on my plate right now."

"Really? From here it looks empty. You sure vacuumed up those eggs."

"They were good."

My father reaches over for one of my toast crusts, folds it into his mouth.

"Old habit," he says. "I always used to eat your leftovers when you were little. Hated to waste the food."

"I remember."

"Did it bother you?"

"No. Felt like we were doing the job together."

My father pours us more coffee from the glass carafe.

"Wish we'd done more family things. Work never seems to slow up. Maybe someday. Like that song. Remember?"

"Little boy blue and the man in the moon."

"Hey, have you been doing shifts for Tony's kid?"

"As many as I can get."

"I know you guys aren't pals."

"Not exactly."

"I don't know why not. His dad says he's a lot more mature now, and you're both interested in the arts."

"You and Roy Cohn are both lawyers."

"Point taken. Do you need any money?"

"I mean, if you need to unload some."

My father plucks two folded twenties from his shirt pocket.

"Good thing you had it right there," I say.

"Are you doing okay?" he says with a kind of concerned frown.

"It's been kind of a hard week."

"Tell me about it," he says, but I'm not quite sure he means precisely that. Still, I'm about to launch into a rundown of the last few days and ask my father for his thoughts on Mr. Massad's legal situation, how Mr. Massad might get paid what he's owed by the blond idiot whose people possibly sent a giant ponytailed maniac to harass his son, the same maniac who might have killed Toad, and I'm just figuring out how to explain it when the wall phone rings. My father snatches up the receiver.

"Yeah? Oh, hey, Mike. Yeah? That's what he said? Well, the fucko is in for it. We'll nail him on precedent. Slam dunk, my friend. Chocolate thunder. Hold on a sec."

129

My father covers the mouthpiece with his palm.

"Hang around for a while?"

"Sorry," I say. "I've got to get back."

"Okay, kid. To be continued."

My father leans over the counter, kisses my forehead.

My mother gives me a lift to the bus stop. She's bundled up in her old red loden coat, her hair under a pale silk scarf. She's got her movie-star sunglasses on for the occasion, guides her Buick Skylark through the morning's slush and glare.

"That was fun last night," she says.

"Yeah."

"It's nice to see you once in a while."

"Same here."

My hope is for a quick, quiet ride, but it looks like we're going to talk.

"I know we've had our battles, honey, but I want you to know I'm behind you. Don't get trapped in a place like this."

"Mom, you have a good life."

"Don't take it the wrong way, Jonathan. Your father and I are doing all right. I don't even care that much about the affair anymore. It's just that we were kidding ourselves that we'd have equal careers or something."

"You have a career. You're an art teacher. And you volunteer at the newspaper."

"I'm a babysitter with a crafts closet. And it's nineteen ninety-three. Nobody cares about a bunch of middle-aged feminists and their rag."

"I do."

"That's nice. I'm glad I raised you to be such a bad liar."

"Mom."

"But I guess if I could have accomplished more, I would have."

"It was tough for women. Still is."

"I know you understand that. Support the women around you."

"I do."

"Good. As for your music, well, what do I know about what's going on? At least you are following your bliss, as they say."

"It's not always blissful," I say.

"Believe me, I get it. But still. It's good to do interesting things, especially when you are young. Do fun things. Kiss a lot of people. Fondle them. Sometimes fondling is better than intercourse, and with all of the diseases—"

"I get it!"

"But only if they want to do fondling. The fondling has to be mutual."

"I understand, Mom."

"I've kissed my share of people, you know. When your father and I were separated all those years ago, I went on some crazy dates. I even dated Bink Tellman once."

"Really? Does Helen know?"

"Of course."

"Did you like him?"

"He was kind of kooky. I really couldn't understand that book. What was it? *Embargo*? Though the movie was good. Oh, here we are. Let me just pull over. I'll wait for the bus so you don't have to stand in the cold."

"Thanks."

I switch on the radio. News rides low static. The president and the first lady have settled into the White House. The Soyuz

131

TM-16 rocket has launched, headed for the former Soviet space station. Retired Supreme Court Justice Thurgood Marshall has died.

"They're all dying," my mother says.

"Who?"

"People."

"My friend died," I say.

"What?" my mother says.

"His name was Toad."

"Oh, honey. What happened? Was he on drugs? I get so worried about—"

"He was murdered."

"You're kidding. Murdered? Do the police know who did it?"

"Not yet."

"Jonathan, that neighborhood you're in. I keep saying, you have to get one of those bars for the door, and that rod that sticks in the floor. The standard lock is not enough."

"It wasn't the neighborhood. By which you mean what, anyway?"

"You're the one who said the police don't know who did it."

"They're working on it!"

"So it was probably some robber. I'm not saying what kind. It's not their fault. It's the system. But it doesn't mean you have to bare your throat to them."

"Nobody's baring!" I say.

"Sweetie, don't shout."

"I'm not shouting!"

"I said please don't shout!"

"She shouted," I mutter.

My mother stares out the windshield.

"Here's your bus."

"Thanks for the ride."

I guess I should have walked to the stop. Such is the way with us. Maybe it will always be like this, at least until we forgive each other for a crime neither of us could ever name.

EIGHTEEN

I'm only back in the Rock Rook for a few minutes when Corrina calls, asks me to come over. She has a surprise.

She greets me at her door with a jelly jar full of dark red liquid.

"Is that what I think it is?" I say.

"My proprietary mix."

Corrina grins, leads me into the kitchen, which is swathed in sheets of tinfoil. Shards of stained glass lean up on the wall behind the sink. A large wooden crucifix hangs on a cabinet door, the ornately carved Christ shiny, bony. A photograph of another man's head, clipped from a magazine, is taped over the face of Jesus.

"Is that the landlord from *Three's Company*?" I say.

"Mr. Roper," Corrina says, screws a camcorder into a tripod.

"Is he of religious significance to you?"

"That's a silly question."

I glance again at the crucifix, the stained glass.

"Is it?"

"I need you to take off your clothes now," Corrina says.

"You first."

"No, me last. Right now we are making art and you will be the naked one."

"Okay," I say, strip down to my briefs.

"Are those Underoos?"

"No, they're just colorful. Two bucks for a pack of five. They're from the defective bin."

"What's defective about them?"

"I'm not sure yet."

"Well, you get what you pay for. Now take them off. And put this wig on."

I'm not certain I comprehend the grander narrative, but my task, as laid out by Corrina, is to enter this silvered kitchen of a Kingdom Come in the buff after donning a hair piece that approximates the chestnut locks of *Three's Company* star John Ritter. I will behold the crucifix, enact a classic double take, fall to my knees, douse myself in blood from the jelly jar, and scoot back out the door, whereupon I am instructed to scream like crazy.

"Won't the neighbors complain?"

"Probably not."

"I can't deal with another visit from the cops."

"It'll be fine. People make all kinds of rackets in this building."

"Okay."

"So, are you ready for your close-up?"

"Tony the Turd might appreciate this," I say.

"Who?"

"A man of the cinema. May I ask you a question?"

"Shoot."

"I mean, I think I know what you're getting at with this piece."

"Really?"

"Or maybe not. But still, why *Three's Company*? Why not any other seventies sitcom?"

"I'm Catholic."

"So?"

"It's in the title. The Trinity."

"That's why Mr. Roper is on the cross? He's the Son?"

"No, Jack Tripper is the Son, obviously. Mr. Roper is the Deceiver. The Dark Prince. His visage is momentarily occluding that of Jesus."

"Then who is the Father?"

"Janet, of course."

"And Chrissy is the Holy Ghost."

"You do understand."

"What about Mrs. Roper? Or Larry?"

"Lesser demons."

"And Mr. Furley?"

"That's a different cosmology."

"But still, why?"

"Why what? Why am I making a short, quasi-parodic, wholly passionate Kenneth Anger–inspired avant-garde feminist short film exploring the ways my relationship to television and organized religion have deformed my sexuality and womanhood?"

"Yeah, that."

"None of your fucking beeswax. Are you ready?"

"I think so."

"Don't spill the blood until it's time. We have a limited supply."

"Okay."

"Great. By the way, I really appreciate this. You're the only one I could find to do it."

"You asked a lot of people?"

"Don't look so disappointed."

"I'm not."

"All right, then. Action!"

Next thing I'm on my knees, mid-scream, Corrina's blood pouring down my face, when the door buzzes.

"Shit!" Corrina says. "Shit! Okay, cut! Save the blood! We might have to do it again."

I tip the cup back up.

"So fucking typical," Corrina says.

"Expecting somebody?"

Corrina reaches for the intercom beside the door.

"Hello?"

"Corrina, it's me," says a voice with a vague European accent, though the vagueness is more a matter of my ignorance than the accent itself. "I'm coming up."

"Who's that?" I say.

"Mateo."

"Your roommate?"

"My husband."

I recall the other day at the Stop Pit, the teasing query from Trancine.

"Like ex-husband?" I say.

"No. Husband."

"Estranged?"

"Not really."

"So it's sort of an open thing?"

"Not officially."

"Okay, just trying to understand the situation."

"It's not great."

"Well, you don't have to let him in," I say.

"He has a key."

"Then why'd he buzz?"

"Courtesy."

I've barely got my long johns back on when the front door crashes open and a lanky guy with heavy hair and motorcycle leathers strides through the living room. He stops at the edge of the kitchen, looks me up and down.

"Mateo," he says.

"Jack Shit," I say, and for the first time I feel like the genuine owner of my name.

"Where's Corrina?"

"Right here," she says, slips in past Mateo, stands behind me. "We were working. But, of course, your timing is impeccable."

"That's the sarcasm tone again," Mateo says. "You know it's tricky for me. Also I just got off a plane. My brain is eggs. Give me a break."

"Oh, sure, a break. Because if there is anybody who deserves one, it's you."

"You know," I say. "I'm going to go now. Give you guys a chance to catch up."

"No, Jack Shit," Mateo says. "Better you stay."

"Better I go," I say.

I grab my clothes and bolt out of there, finish dressing in the stairwell.

NINETEEN

It's gotten even colder and I've left one of my layers, my treasured Epcot Center sweater, at Corrina's. Now I'm shivering outside Cutwolf's place. Passers-by throw odd looks, speed up. The entrance to Cutwolf's is right on the street, a frosted-glass door behind a retractable metal gate. I shake the gate to rouse him. The door rattles open, but instead of Cutwolf standing there, it's the Egyptian god Anubis, all loincloth and jackal's head.

"Can I help you?" Anubis says, crosses his arms over his bare chest.

The loincloth, I realize on closer inspection, is a large diaper, and the canine visage is a fairly realistic party mask, more wolf than anything.

"Cut?"

The mask slides up.

"Jonathan. Is that you?"

"Who the fuck else would it be? And you better stop calling me Jonathan. *Craig.*"

"Sorry. Jack. Are you okay?"

"Why wouldn't I be okay?"

"Because you've got blood all over your face and you're wearing a— What is that? A pageboy wig?"

"Well, you're wearing a fucking diaper and a wolf mask."

"I was waiting for somebody."

"Who?"

"I can't tell you."

"Let me in," I say.

Cutwolf moves aside and I step down into his dark hovel. It's not unlike the Rock Rook, with a mattress on the floor and some books and records in milk crates. He's got a little practice amp on an upturned wooden box, a toilet, and a tiny sink in the corner. The building's super fashioned this cell from an old storefront, rents it out behind the landlord's back. That's why Cutwolf has no phone but a glass door and a metal gate. It's not really a residence.

I flip a spare milk crate, sit down.

Cutwolf flops down on his mattress, lights a cigarette. He flicks ash into a seashell full of butts beside his pillow.

"Wait," Cut says. "Is that your blood?"

"It's Corrina's."

"Is she okay?"

"She's fine. It was for this movie she's making."

"A movie, huh?"

"Yeah."

"Well, you look pretty fucked up."

"I do? What about you?"

"Maybe we should play Artaud's in these getups."

"I like it," I say.

Cutwolf stubs out his cigarette, picks up his guitar, runs some scales.

"Who were you expecting?" I say.

"Just don't tell anyone, okay?"

"I won't."

"Trancine."

"Stop Pit Trancine? She's like fifty years old."

"She's thirty-five."

"Her band used to open for the Ramones and Mink De-Ville, for God's sake."

"She was a kid."

"How long have you two been at it?"

"Not long."

"What's with the diaper? Or the mask?"

"Just started as a little joke. But now it's, like, I don't know . . . a thing."

"I suppose Hod has no idea."

"He's a good guy," Cutwolf says, "but he's kind of dumb and actually not really a good guy. Not to her."

"Is he violent?"

"Doesn't hit her. But he's a fucker. Gets drunk and just harangues her. Makes her cry."

"Maybe because she cheats on him."

"You don't know the deal."

"No, you're right," I say. "I don't know a goddamn thing about anything. I don't know why Trancine is cheating on Hod, or why Hod is a prick to her. I don't know why Hera would rather play in Thorazine than the Shits, even with all of our problems. I don't know why you keep major secrets from me. I definitely don't know what the hell I'm doing with my life. But most of all I don't know why I can't find the fucking Earl, or my bass!"

"I don't know where the Earl is either," Cutwolf says. "But his dad filed a missing person report."

"He did? How do you know that?"

"That cop came by asking questions about Toad again. He told me."

141

"Fielden?"

"Yeah."

"So now what?"

"I don't know. We wait."

Cut lights another cigarette, sticks it in his headstock.

"Trancine's coming?" I ask.

"She's supposed to."

"Well, I guess I should go."

"Hey, Jonathan—"

"Jack! My name is Jack Shit. Get it straight, you ridiculous motherfucker!"

I stand, kick the seashell. Cig butts bounce on the concrete floor.

"Okay, Jack, calm down!"

I seethe for a moment, walk to the sink in the corner, wash the blood off my face.

"Hey, Jack?"

"What?"

"I'm thinking for Artaud's, if we do play the show, we open with either 'Orbit City Comedown' or 'Orange Julius Rosenberg.' I mean, 'Rosenberg' has that drum intro that might be cool, but I was also thinking 'Comedown' might be the way in. What do you think? Or maybe 'Chives and Whiskey.'"

"I thought you hated 'Chives and Whiskey.' When we wrote that song you said it was too cowpunk. As a matter of fact, you said it reminded you of the Saddle Sores and that you secretly hated the Saddle Sores."

"I've evolved," Cutwolf says, slides down his mask.

I study myself in the mirror above the sink, adjust my wig. Maybe I'll wear it awhile.

"Whatever," I say, unlatch the glass door, yank the gate aside.
"I'm leaving."

"But, Jack—"

I book out of there, head for the Jew-Hater's bar.

The room is dark, as usual, even with the year-round strings of
blinking Christmas lights, and mostly empty. Gleb sets me up
with a bourbon and I nod across the horseshoe bar at a guy I
don't know in an Annihilation of the Soft Left T-shirt.

Gleb flips a coaster for my drink onto the scarred walnut.

"Friend of yours?" Gleb says.

"No," I say.

"He's like you. Another godless money-grubbing Bolshevik
with his oh-so-special God."

"It never got more coherent than that, did it, Gleb?"

"If it ain't broke," Gleb says, moves away.

Our eyes meet again across the bar. The guy does look a
little familiar.

"Nice shirt," I say.

"Thanks."

"You like that band?"

"Wouldn't say that, exactly," the guy says. "I played in it."

"No shit," I say. "Me too."

We laugh.

"There must be dozens of us in a ten-block radius."

"No doubt," I say.

It takes a few drinks but soon me and this guy, whose
name is Gary, wade deep into bogs of shared history. We trade
our favorite Toad stories, his ceaseless crotch-clawing, his

vacillation between brands of mint jelly, the doomed gigs he booked for us in upstate VFW halls where yowling about Ike Eisenhower's "fascist little titties," as one of Toad's torch songs had it, could get you jumped in the john. Worse, in some ways, were the shows in dumpling houses or red-sauce joints in New Jersey or Pennsylvania (what kind of easy-listening demo had Toad offered for the bait and switch?), because the owners would try to be polite, even while their clientele poured into the parking lot with their hands clamped over their ears.

Gary and I compare dates. We missed each other by a year or two. He was kind of a legend, the guitarist with only one thumb. I clock his hand now and see that it's the same guy, though I can't recall if I ever heard how he lost it. Toad rarely talked about past band members, and when he did you could hardly understand him for the froth in his mouth. Anyone not playing with him at a given moment was a running dog, a scab, a traitor, a rat bastard.

"What are you doing these days?" I say.

"I work at this photo lab. But I'm thinking of going back to my hometown for a while. Get my shit straight. I've kind of had it."

"I hear you."

We sit and sip our drinks. I'm not sure why I haven't mentioned Toad's death, except that it's almost an eerie comfort to pretend he's alive. Still, I have to let Gary know.

"Listen," I say. "I've got some news."

"About Toad?"

"Yeah."

"I heard. It's all around. I just didn't feel like—"

"Me either," I say.

Now the bar's vinyl-upholstered door slurps open. Corrina is beautiful in a fake foxtail under the red exit light.

"You dumb fuck," she says. "I've been looking all over for you."

"Where's Mateo?"

"I don't know. Or care. I mean I do know. He's home. Come with me. I want to take you somewhere."

"I don't know how to start trusting you again."

"Did you trust me before? There will be free drinks."

"I'll go," Gary says.

"No, just Jack."

"Take care," I say to Gary.

"Back at you, man. And remember. Don't be a kulak. Make your own Popsicles."

Corrina and I walk west. I stop at the corner, lean up on the lamppost.

"I can't," I say.

"Can't what?"

"Come with you."

"Why?"

For the second time in a few days, I sob on Corrina's shoulder.

"It's okay," she says, guides me to the curb, sits me down on the cold, wet concrete. "What is it?"

I say some words through snot and tears. I'm not quite sure what I stutter, but it's something about Toad and the Earl and fear and futility. I tell her about the missing person report.

"Maybe the police will find him," she says.

"Fuck the police," I say.

"I love that song."

"Me too."

"Look, Jack, I like you. But you have to stop the crying shit."

"But I'm sharing my feelings. I thought women, especially, appreciated that."

"To a point. After a while, though, it's just more work."

"Okay."

"But I know I've met you during a crazy week. I'll give you a pass for now. Also, if it makes you feel better, I only asked three people to do the video piece before you."

"That does make me feel better."

"Good. Now let's go to the gallery."

"Where?"

"To where the other half hangs out."

"The other half?"

"The other half of me. The life I'm supposed to be living."

"Now I'm confused."

"Good."

TWENTY

A light snow falls by the time we hit SoHo. The sign in the gallery window reads PETER APOSTLE ARTS. A throng mills on the sidewalk in swirls of smoke. Limos idle near the curb.

"Big crowd," I say. "Isn't it Sunday night?"

"That's Apostle's trademark."

"This guy's a big deal?"

"One of the biggest."

"Do you know him?"

"I know the artist. She used to be my best friend."

"Used to?"

"Look, just don't leave me alone in there."

"Okay," I say.

We push our way inside, stand pressed together in a throb of bodies, some of them swaddled in business suits, others in rich fabrics cut to more bohemian codes. Guests chatter, laugh, squeal. The long white chamber swallows and regurgitates the din.

Corrina and I come upon a sculpture, a rusted metal music stand placed inside an inflatable kiddie pool filled with chunks of purple Jell-O. Strips of spangled black leather dangle from the scrolled wings of the stand. A shredded violin bow, stained red, rests against some sheet music open in the tray. The title of the musical composition, and presumably this work of art, is printed in heavy Gothic font: KICK OUT THE JUDEN, MUTTERFICKER!

The name of the artist and the show is stenciled in tasteful gray on the wall: MONICA SNELL: INTERROGATING THE INTERVENTION.

Voices rise around us.

"Peter is very excited. Says he's going to get her into the Biennial."

"The show is so brilliant. It's definitely time to intervene in the interrogation."

"I believe it's the other way around."

"Sorry."

A couple brushes past us, an elegant woman with short black hair and a dark-browed middle-aged guy in a blazer and blue jeans.

"There they are!" the woman exclaims in a British accent. "See, I told you I wouldn't disappoint you, Jeffrey!"

The woman waves across the room at two blonde girls in miniskirts. The girls, who look more like eighth-grade kids on a field trip than sophisticated gallerygoers, wave back. The man grins, quivers.

"Oh God," Corrina says, clutches my arm. "There she is."

Near the sculpture, circled by admirers, stands a young woman.

"Who?" I say.

"Monica," Corrina says, maybe a little too loudly, because the woman turns and seems to spot us. A sour look crosses her face, but she recovers with a smile, cuts through the crowd and around her rusted monument to National Socialism, classic American dessert food, and, for whatever reason, the Motor City Five. She trots over to Corrina, hugs her.

"Rinny! I'm so psyched you're here!"

"Monica, this is so awesome! I'm so excited for you!"

"Thanks!"

"Oh," Corrina says. "This is Jack. Do you know the Shits? The band? I think you'd really like them."

"Cool," Monica says. "I don't know them, but I've been doing a multimedia project with these really amazing musicians. Maybe you know them, Jack. They're called Mongoose Civique?"

"Yeah, sure, I know those guys," I say.

"Then you must have heard the news. They just signed a huge contract with Geffen Records."

"They did?" I say, feel my voice rising. "Those fucking poseurs!"

"Oh," Monica says.

The news makes me queasy. Corrina squeezes my hand, a hidden consolation. Certain truths, like the fact that in this twisted world it's the charlatans who emerge victorious, still hurt, but now is no time for self-pity. Later tonight, perhaps, will be a good time.

"Just kidding," I say now quickly. "Wait, did you say Mongoose Civique? Oh, I thought you said— Anyway, I must be confused. By the way, I really like this piece here."

"Thanks."

"Are you an MC5 fan?" I say.

"Who?"

"The Motor City Five? You know, kick out the jams, motherfuckers! You must be a fan to use their phrase. Did you know the Stooges used to be their opening band? It was real revolution shit. Not like Mongoose . . . or, whatever. 'Rama lama, fa fa fa. Brothers and sisters, I want to tell you something. I hear a lot of talk from a lot of honkeys, sitting on a lot of money, telling me they're the high society, but if you ask me—'"

"Jack?" Corrina says.

"Sorry," I say. "I get carried away. They had the best banter."

"Yeah, no," Monica says. "I was just working off a well-known generic phrase from the sixties counterculture."

"Generic?" I say.

"Rinny," Monica says. "I just can't get over how great it is that you came tonight."

"I'm really glad I did."

Monica grasps Corrina's arms, tugs her close.

"I'll just say it straight out," Monica says. "I want to be friends again. You helped me so much. I mean all that time, all those conversations. Half of these pieces should have your name on them too."

"I'm just so proud of you, Monica. You really did it."

Corrina's green eyes sparkle with what I'm beginning to sense isn't joy.

"I'll call you tomorrow, Rinny," Monica says, hugs Corrina again, turns, plunges into a fresh cluster of supplicants.

Corrina takes a long breath, smiles.

"She seems nice," I say.

"Thieving cunt," she says.

"Or that. Should we look at the rest of the show?"

"No," Corrina says. "I've seen most of these pieces before. When I thought of them."

"So, do *you* like the MC5?"

"'I hear a lot of talk by a lot of honkeys, sitting on a lot of money, telling me they're the high society, but if you ask me— *this is the high society!*'"

"Exactly!"

150

"Let's go."

"Okay, Rinny."

"No," says Corrina. "Corrina. Always."

"Deal."

We're about to leave when there is a commotion at the front of the gallery. A group in dark suits cuts through the room. Flash-bulbs pop around them and a pair of bodyguards carves a path for a tall man with a pasty face and yellow hair. He swivels as he walks, nods in either direction. A woman with a notebook slides up to him. His jutting lower lip bobs with short bursts of speech. I hear snatches of it: "Great . . . Very good . . . Fantastic . . . The art . . . There's a real market for it . . . and don't forget Picasso, or even the caves. Yes, a lot of people love the cave painting, but it's hard to transport that stuff, that's why there's not much of a market for it. . . . This show, yes, very nice. What do I think it means? I think it means people are excited. Peter Apostle is a good friend. We see him in Florida. A lot of people are saying he's a genius."

"That's—" I start to say.

"Of course he has to make an appearance," a woman beside me says. "Just here to do his Page Six lap."

"What a circus," Corrina says.

The star and his entourage are a few feet from the far wall when they pivot together like a trained troupe, or school of fish, wriggle back through the crush toward the gallery door. The star's gaze seems to fall on the quivering man and the British woman.

"Jeffrey! Always with the jeans!"

Now the leading *artiste* of the business deal, the man Bink Tellman called a symptom of moral and civic decay, turns his watery blue eyes on me.

"Donald Trump!" I shout. "Show us the way!"

The man nods and seems about to reply when one of the bodyguards wedges himself between us. I stare at whorls of dark hair sprouting out of an open-collared dress shirt, look up the tree-trunk neck to the titanic head, the long silver ponytail.

"You!" I say.

Mounce's eyes flash, but I can't tell if they recognize me. His mammoth palm shoves me away. I nearly knock over *Kick Out the Juden, Mutterficker!* as I skid to the floor. A gallery assistant grabs my arm.

"What are you doing?" she says. "Be careful!"

"Sorry," I say, pull free. Mounce and the others are already at the door. I push through the throng, but as I get to the sidewalk, the taillights of their limo shrink away into the frozen night.

Corrina rushes out, jogs up.

"Are you okay?"

"That was him!"

"Who?"

"The guy Hod saw with the Earl! Who maybe killed Toad!"

"Are you sure?"

"That was definitely the fucker who had my bass at King Snake. I don't know if he recognized me. I've got to find him. I think I know where to look."

"Be careful," Corrina says.

"Aren't you coming?"

"I don't think I will be much help. And I have to go home."

"To Mateo."

"I have to tell him to leave."

"Will he listen?"

"Yes. I think so."

Corrina kisses me.

"I can reshoot the scene if you need me."

"I think we got it."

"Good."

"I lied," she says. "You were the only person I asked to play blood-drenched Jack Tripper."

"Why me?"

"I could tell right off that you'd bring the right commitment to the role."

"You have to leave everything out on the bitching floor," I tell her. "I believe that."

"No doubt. I mean, shit, you're still wearing the wig."

TWENTY-ONE

After I leave Corrina, I find a pay phone, call Dyl, tell him to meet me at the Pinsk. A public place seems safer. It's early evening and the streets are pretty crowded for a cold night. Our Lady of the Sealed Works waddles by, nods hello. I pass some people in line outside a tenement doorway. They are a varied bunch, some in thick, respectable overcoats, others shivering in zip-ups and jeans, or in rags. They look like professors, busboys, hairdressers, antiques sellers, janitors, clerks, kids. A melting pot of scag-scoring.

A man in a shiny black jacket shouts at them to straighten the line, a schoolteacher on cafeteria duty. The customers approach the vestibule, clutch their bills. How many times has the Earl stood here, jumpy, aching, nervous, a poem of blood pain dancing on his lips, the dope sickness a net dropped over his body, the dope a knife for slashing his way free?

We watched him get worse and worse. We had our own problems, but we might have tried harder to stop the unspooling. Did we fear that once he got clean, he might find better friends and bandmates, desert us? Sometimes I wonder.

Now he's gone all the same.

"End of the line," the chaperone snaps.

"Huh?"

"Get on the end of the line."

154

"No, not . . ."

I scurry off toward the Pinsk.

Near the entrance I hear Dyl's voice.

"Jack!"

"Hey," I say, turn.

"Nice wig," he says. "I almost didn't . . ."

I pull the wig off, stuff it in my coat pocket.

"Let's go in," I say.

Dyl nods. It's warm and bright in the diner, a dream of butter-yellow Formica. I spot Hera and Cutwolf. They've staked out a booth and look deep into something unpleasant, plates of pierogi, onion rings untouched between them.

"After you called, Cutwolf came by," Dyl whispers. "Said he was meeting Hera. I suggested here. Figured the more of us, the better."

"Fine," I say, sidle up to the booth. Hera's eyes are wet and red. She and Cutwolf light cigarettes, slump back.

"Sit down," Cutwolf says.

Dyl and I slide in on either side.

"You okay?" I say to Hera.

"Yeah, I guess."

"Thorazine broke up," Cutwolf says, the feigned sorrow in his voice not quite tamping down the glee.

"Well, actually, Wallach and I broke up, and then he kicked me out of the band."

"It's just the two of you," I say. "How could he kick you out?"

"Why don't you just kick him out?" Cutwolf says.

"He was Thorazine first."

"Fuck him," Cutwolf says. "He's a cretin."

"No, he's not," Hera says. "There's no point in pretending. I wasn't at his level anyway."

"His level?" Cutwolf says. "What level? He's nowhere. He's a bore. He's not punk rock and he's not even one of those lame virtuosos riding arpeggios up his own ass either. But you, Hera, you are a killer drummer, fucking smart and tough, and you're also . . ."

We all wait for Cutwolf to finish his sentence. It almost sounds like he's about to say something personal, or even declare his love. Maybe he does have those feelings for her. The more I dwell on certain moments from the past, the ways I'd sometimes catch Cutwolf looking at Hera in the practice room or at the Stop Pit, the more I'm convinced this could be true. Has his inability to speak his heart driven him into the arms of a middle-aged woman who makes him wear a diaper and a wolf mask? Or is that an unrelated phenomenon? People are complicated.

"Also what?" Hera says.

"You're also a good songwriter," Cutwolf says.

"Thanks."

They both suck hard on their smokes, exhale, look over at Dyl and me.

"Any news about Alan?" Hera says.

"No," I say. "But I may have a lead."

I tell them about the opening at Peter Apostle's gallery, the entourage, Mounce.

"We've got to find that bastard," Cutwolf says.

"We need to be careful, though," Hera says. "He sounds dangerous."

"Oh, he's definitely dangerous," I say. "But fuck it. And fuck him. And fuck the fucks he works for. We've got to track him down, find out what he knows about the Earl."

"Or what he did to him," Dyl says.

"We don't know anything about that," Cutwolf says.

"Shouldn't we call the cops?" Hera says.

"We can call Fielden," I say. "I left him a message before."

"I'll try him," Cutwolf says, heads for the pay phone near the register. I snatch up an onion ring.

"I'm starving," I say.

Vesna used to rag on me for using that word when genuine hunger plagued huge swaths of the world.

"Fine," I told her. "But don't forget that just last week you said you'd kill for the boots you saw in that window on St. Marks."

"So?" Vesna said.

"You don't think murder is a global problem?"

The look on Vesna's face should have told me we didn't have much longer to go as a couple. Maybe she was already humping that Ken doll from Mongoose Civique. Vesna must have known about the big record deal when I saw them at the Thorazine show. Goddamn corporate puppets. Not that I would turn down a contract from Geffen. But only so our subversive music could reach more ears. Mongoose Civique, though, that's just consumption pop with a fuzz pedal.

Cutwolf returns, slips into the booth.

"What's on your mind?" he says.

"What?" I say.

"Your lips were moving."

"Oh, sorry. I was just—"

"Thinking," Hera says. "We know. We've been around you enough."

"Did you know Mongoose Civique signed with Geffen?"

"Are you surprised?" Cutwolf says, laughs.

"I guess I was."

"Scruffy moppets in vintage cardigans playing crunchy power pop sign a record deal! Stop the presses!"

"Fine," I say. "What did Fielden say?"

"He said to sit tight. He's just getting off his shift."

"Meantime," Hera says, "I think we should tell Crystal we can't play Artaud's on Saturday. Better to tell her now than flake out."

"But we don't know," Cutwolf says. "Maybe the Earl's been holed up somewhere. Maybe he'll come back. Just appear. A mess, I'm sure, but that never stopped him from singing before."

"Or maybe he's dead in an alley," Dyl says.

"Or in a garbage can," I say, remember what the desk sergeant at the precinct house asked me about all those months ago, the downtown dumbass with his throat cut. Did Mounce do that with his Gerber combat blade?

"Stop!" Hera says. "This isn't productive. We need to decide about the show."

We go around like this a few more times, argue the pros and cons of canceling Saturday, and also accuse each other of not taking our front man's decline seriously enough, and then Fielden walks into the Pinsk. Today's look is less Serpico than latter-day Springsteen: leather jacket, white T-shirt, blue jeans, engineer boots. Is he daring us to comment on the red bandanna tied in a neat fold across his forehead?

He shoves himself into the booth, pushes Dyl into Cutwolf, Cutwolf into the wall.

"I see the whole crime-fighting club showed up. Nice."

I grin at the crack, proceed.

"Detective, I think I've made a break in the case."

"A break?" Fielden snorts.

"Isn't that how you guys say it?" I say.

"Say what? What are you trying to do, Jack? Who are you trying to be?"

"I'm trying to be the person who figures out what happened to his friend. I saw Heidy Mounce."

"How do you know it was him?"

"He recognized him from the other day," Dyl says. "When he brought Jack's bass into King Snake."

"And who the hell are you?" Fielden says.

"He works in the guitar store," I say.

"I do work there," Dyl says, "but I'm mainly a musician. And a sound engineer. And sometimes I tech for—"

"Enough with the fucking résumé, buddy," Fielden says, points at me. "Just say your piece."

"My piece, Detective, is that there is no question in my mind that the big dude with the giant head and the silver ponytail, who I saw with my bass at King Snake and who mentioned Alan by name while we were there, and who I also recognized at a recent art opening, and who the Denim Ghoul called Mounce, which was a name you recognized as belonging to a man whose physical description, as provided by me, matched the one in your memory—Wait, where was I? Okay, the point is that this guy, Detective, is the same goon who leaned on the Earl's father to drop his complaint about unpaid labor for a construction job and was the last person to see the Earl, having left the Stop Pit with him on Wednesday night, and is, in all probability, the man who murdered Toad Molotov. That's it. That's the break. Find Mounce, and we find the Earl, and Toad's killer, and maybe even my bass guitar. And we *can* find Mounce, because we know who his boss is."

"Donald Fuckhead Trump," Dyl says, throws me a nod.

"Well, I'm sure there are a load of assholes in the chain of command between them," I say. "But yeah."

I pick up an onion ring, wedge it into my mouth. Fielden reaches for one of Hera's Kools, lights it, takes a long draw.

"That it, Cannon?" he says, which is kind of mean if you know that show from the '70s with the obese detective, but I let it slide.

"That's it."

"Okay, then I've got one question for you," Fielden says. "Who or what the fuck is the Denim Ghoul?"

"Just a guy I know in the neighborhood."

"Who happened to be there to ID Mounce?"

"Said he was a killer," Dyl says. "Said he'd killed more than a few of us."

"Us who?"

"We don't know," I say. "Other neighborhood people, maybe?"

"He goes by 'the Denim Ghoul'?" Fielden says.

"No, that's just my secret nickname for him."

"What's his real name?"

"I don't know."

"No, of course you don't. Why would you bother learning something like that? It's not like any of this is real. It's just a movie you get to be in for a while."

"What the hell does that mean?" Cutwolf says.

"I think you know," Fielden says. "Look, I've been nice. But I'm getting tired."

"I'm giving you the doer," I say.

"The what? Are you ordering me a scotch?"

"You guys don't say 'doer'?" I say. "It was on a show. Whatever. Mounce killed Toad Molotov. Don't you get it? You can clear the case!"

"Were you this obnoxious," Fielden says, "that time you turned yourself in to the precinct house for railing carpet cleaner in your apartment?"

"What?"

"I found a file on you. We keep notes on local freaks."

"I knew it," I say. "You guys do care."

"He was having a difficult time," Dyl says. "There were baby rats in his shower curtain."

"Enough of this bullshit about Mounce," Fielden says. "These fantasies. Just let it go. Walk away. Do your thing. Aren't you a band? Don't you have any gigs to play?"

"We do," Hera says. "We're playing Artaud's Garage on Saturday."

"So, it's decided?" Cutwolf says.

"There you go," Fielden says. "You do your job. We'll do ours."

"If you were doing your job," I say, "you'd be busting Heidy Mounce right now."

"Oh yeah?"

Fielden pops to his feet, grabs my collar, leans in, whispers.

"Listen, you stupid prick. You need to lay off, pronto. These are people you should spend your whole life steering clear of. You get to live in your sweet, protected world, your little dirt-bag Disneyland, because other people have arranged it for you. Because it's good for business all around. You move in and pretend it's nineteen seventy-six, but it's not. You're just yuppies, but with torn jeans and track marks instead of oxford shirts and squash injuries. Actually, I'm sure some of you have both. I know who you are. I went to college with people like you."

"Where'd you go to college?" Hera asks.

"Amherst," Fielden says.

"Bay Ridge boy," I say.

"That's right."

"You got out."

"I wasn't trying to escape. Just get a fucking education."

"My sister went to Amherst," Hera says. "Calliope Bern-berger? What year were you?"

"It doesn't matter what year," Fielden says. "What matters

is— Calliope? Yeah, I knew her. We . . . I mean, we all— It doesn't fucking matter, okay? All you need to understand is that you are living in a goddamn amusement park that is pretty much safe if you stay within the perimeter, stick to your coffee shops, your bars, your clubs, even your cop spots. But do not fuck with the people who really belong here, whether they are slinging dope on the corner or closing real estate deals in office towers. Not to mention all the hardworking civilians just trying to get through the day. Do you understand? Just play out your artsy-fartsy dream until you get too old or too tired of being broke and mediocre and it's time for the next batch of fools to roll in. As for your buddy, I'm sure he was a nice kid once, but it sounds like he fell off the cliff. Happens. It's a shame. But as long as there aren't too many, it does add to the flavor of the place. Though lately there seems to be a glut. And the saddest thing is an uptown junkie."

"They're only into it," I say, "because they hurt so much inside."

"What?"

"Oh, I thought you were quoting something."

"I wasn't quoting anything, you miserable fuck. Now I'll just say it one more time. Stop playing cop."

Fielden stabs out his cigarette in a soggy pierogi, stands, strides out of the Pinsk. Nobody speaks for a moment.

"Dyl," I say. "How's your van running?"

"Wouldn't drive it across the country."

"What about past Fourteenth Street?"

"Should be fine."

TWENTY-TWO

We wait outside the Pinsk for Dyl to drive up with his van. It's an old red Econoline he got from his cousin and uses for man-with-a-van gigs and to help friends ferry gear. He pulls up, Bollocks, his rottweiler, in the passenger seat. We know better than to try to oust Bollocks. We pile into the back, settle onto heaps of quilted moving blankets.

"Strap in," Dyl says. "Might be a bumpy ride."

"What fucking straps?" Cutwolf says.

We cruise north up Third Avenue past Fourteenth Street, and I realize that apart from the few times I took the train to Port Authority to catch a bus to New Jersey, I haven't been this far uptown in a few years. It's a different city up here, the skyscrapers, the bustle, the glitz. This is the New York I always figured the counterculture was counter to, the New York of Rockettes and Rockefellers, Carnegie Hall and the Carnegie Deli, Jack Dempsey, Leonard Bernstein, King Kong, Greta Garbo, Gloria Vanderbilt, *Miracle on 34th Street*, the miracle at Studio 54, Elaine's, Tiffany, Sardi's, Sparks Steak House, the hidden opulence of the Park Avenue aristocrats. Beyond the borders were other deep worlds in Harlem and the outer boroughs, but this was skyline New York, locus of glamour and greed. Even the squalid Deuce, that gaudy codpiece clamped across the groin of Manhattan, seemed more carnival midway than blighted Gomorrah.

This, at least, was my cozy childhood vision of the metropolis, a swirl of photographs and movie clips, eavesdropped talk and bedtime fantasias, memories of occasional forays into the city with my mother and father for museums, dim sum.

Now we drive into the concrete heart of the isle.

"Where the hell are you going, Dyl?" Cutwolf says.

"We're going to his big building, right?"

"Do you know where it is?"

"Fifth Avenue."

"Turn on Sixtieth," Hera says. "We'll come back down."

"Got it," Dyl says.

We ease up to a stoplight a few blocks south of Central Park.

"Holy shit," Cutwolf says.

"Look at that," I say. "Pull over."

Dyl slides into a curbside spot and we all peer across the street at a shiny black monolith that shoots up from a stepped facade of cubes. The sign above the soft gold entryway reads TRUMP TOWER.

"What now?" Dyl says.

"Let's check it out," I say. "Maybe they know Mounce."

"Sounds like a long shot," Cutwolf says.

"They all work for the same boss," Dyl says.

"So?" Cutwolf says.

"Guys know guys," I say. "And those guys know guys."

"Where'd you pick that up?" Cutwolf says. "SAT prep at the Merritt Heights library?"

"Fuck off," I say, open the van door, hop out.

"I'm coming with you," Hera says.

"Then I'm coming," Cutwolf says.

"No," Hera says. "Stay here with Dyl."

Hera and I hunch against a blast of wind, cross the street. The atrium is warm, suffused with rich, metallic light. A man and woman in matching uniform blazers, groomed and chipper, greet us from behind a desk.

"I'm sorry," the woman says. "The public area is closing now."

"A pity," I say. "My wife was so looking forward to it."

Hera frowns.

"Actually," she says, "we're here on business. With Mister Trump. We're just in from the Phoenix office."

Neither of us, I guess, are very good at this.

"Wonderful," the man says. "Do you have an appointment with somebody in the firm?"

The duo seems to really take us in now. My Salvation Army layers and Hera's industrial parka adorned with rhinestone brooches and vintage British band pins maybe don't mesh with the styles of the building's usual denizens, pinstripe and cashmere types, some of whom move past us in hushed, formal clusters on the way to the escalator.

"Yes," I say. "It should be under the name Mounce."

"Mounce?"

The woman clicks her computer mouse, scans the screen.

"I'm sorry, Mr. Mounce," the woman says.

"Oh, no," I say. "I'm not Mounce. No fucking way."

The man's eyebrow twitches. Hera clutches my arm.

"I'm sorry but there's still nothing here," the woman says.

"Everything okay?"

Another man in the building blazer, older, more managerial, approaches.

"Sure, Terry," the woman says. "We just don't have their appointment in the system."

"How odd," Terry says, scoots back behind the desk, commandeers the keyboard. "What was the name again?"

"They didn't give their names," the woman says. "But they say they are here to see a Mr. Mounce."

"Mounce?" Terry says.

"Heidegger Mounce," Hera says.

"Heidegger, Heidegger," Terry says, peers more closely at the screen. "No, I don't see it in our directory. Interesting name. I'm also sorry to tell you folks that the public area of this building is closing for the night. So, unless there's anything else . . ."

Terry gives us an odd, deadish stare.

"Thanks for your time, Terry," I say.

"It's been a pleasure."

When we get back to the van it's empty and locked.

"Where are they?" I say.

"The fuck, Jack," Hera says.

"What, they don't appreciate a little improv at the Phoenix office?"

"Over here!" Dyl calls. He's got Bollocks on a leash, shivers with Cutwolf under a streetlight.

"Just needed some air. And Bolly needed to piss."

"How did it go in there?" Cutwolf says.

"Pointless," Hera says.

"Maybe not," I say. "Look."

Across the street there's a soft wink of gold as the main door opens. Terry and a pair of large men in matching overcoats step out to the sidewalk. One of them points out Dyl's van. Another scans the avenue and seems to spot us. They walk briskly in our direction.

"Come on," I say. "I think Bollocks needs a nice stroll."

We trot a couple of blocks north toward the corner of the

park, pass the Plaza Hotel. It's dark out now. The hot-pretzel vendors shutter their carts in the moonlight. A small crowd watches a mime in mittens juggle snow globes. Carriage horses snort in the frosty air, nibble carrots from the fists of their drivers, dour-looking men in shabby top hats and cutaway coats.

"Shit, are they following us?" Cutwolf says.

"Keep moving," I say.

Dyl wraps Bollocks's slackened leash once around his wrist and we bound toward the trees. We pass dim shapes of people, evening's stragglers. They jog or power walk or stagger their way out of the park, the slushy path strewn with trash and cigarette butts. Bollocks leads us through an arch where a few people huddle under a torn sleeping bag.

"Isn't that ice rink around here?" Dyl says.

"Wollman," Hera says. "My mother used to take me when I was little."

"Long way from New Canaan," Cutwolf says, laughs.

"Not as long as Idaho," Hera says.

"Ohio."

"Same diff."

"Sometimes I really believe you think that."

"I do."

"Hey, maybe we should find that rink," Dyl says. "Get around some people."

"Good idea," I say.

"This way," says Hera. "Gapstow Bridge. I used to memorize the names."

We cross a stone bridge that spans a small pond. Lights heave into view. Bollocks barks as we trudge toward the rink. The lights, though, deceive. It's just a few security bulbs trained on a locked gate. The rink is empty, full of shadows. An unmanned

Zamboni looms at the far edge. Bollocks leaps at the gate, shakes it.

Behind the gate, a grizzled dude in a park service jacket steps out of a security booth. He lifts his face, his fine, gray mustache, into the light.

"Closed for the evening," he says.

"It's okay, Leonard," a voice behind us says. "You can open up for these people. They are high rollers from Arizona."

It's Terry the manager and his two pals in overcoats.

"We're fine," Hera says. "Just heading home."

"Open the gate, Leonard."

"Really," I say. "We've got to—"

"You are probably well aware," Terry says, "who it was that saved this rink from ruin, paid for all the renovations out of pocket and gave it to the city as a gift. A hero, really."

"Didn't he get all the concessions in exchange?" Hera says. "I remember my father talking about this."

"A good businessman can still be a hero," Terry says. "Capitalism is not a crime. Leonard, open the gate for our friends."

"We're not your friends," I say.

"Leonard!"

The rink guard looks confused.

"Okay."

"And now would be a suitable time to produce your sidearm as well."

"I don't have one," Leonard says.

"Just open the gate, then."

The guard keys open the padlock, swings out the gate.

"Care for a skate?" Terry says. His goons begin to close off our angles.

"Hey!" Cutwolf yells, but Terry and his men grab us, stick

pistols into our backs. Bollocks barks and Terry bashes the dog on the skull with his revolver. Bollocks whimpers, slumps.

"You bastard!" Dyl says.

"Shut up!" Terry hisses.

They hustle us onto the ice. We slide in our sneakers, nearly tumble.

"Sit down," Terry says, steps into the security booth. He picks up a phone and speaks into it, though I can't make out the words.

"It's cold!" Dyl says.

"Sit down!" Terry says as he comes out of the booth and stands at the edge of the rink. We squat. We squat for a while.

"What do you want from us?" I say.

"Shut up!"

We squat some more. The cold tunnels through the soles of my Pumas.

"Is he coming?" one of Terry's men asks.

"Yes," Terry says. "He said to wait here. You know he had a pro tryout? Years ago."

"No shit," the other man says.

Now the gate rattles and we all look up.

"It's open!" Terry calls. "Just push it!"

Mounce looks even bigger under the security light. He wears a garish Christmas sweater and a New York Rangers beanie stretched over his enormous head. He leans on the rink wall, a pair of hockey skates slung around his neck. We watch him tug off his shoes, lace up the blades.

"Figured I'd get in some ice time while I was at it," he says.

"Sure, why not?" Terry says.

"Mounce," I say.

Mounce stares at me for a moment.

"Kid Feces! How you doin'?"

"You know these clowns?" Terry says.

"Just Shit Boy here. That was you at the gallery before, wasn't it? Oh, and here's Poodlehead. I know him too. What are you guys doing uptown, huh? This ain't your business. Shouldn't have dropped my name in the tower."

"I don't know what the hell you think this is," Hera says. "But you and your pals need to let us go now."

"We do?"

"Look, just let us leave," Cutwolf says. "We won't say anything."

"Say anything about what?" Mounce says.

"About anything," Hera says.

"About you and Mr. Massad," I say. "About you and Toad."

Mounce stands, glides out to the center of the rink. He swivels, swoops back toward us with graceful scrapes, leans hard into another turn. His legs pump as he picks up speed, strides the ice like some splendid winter ogre.

"Moves so well for a big fella," Terry mutters.

Mounce circles back, edges into his stop with a lovely spray of ice. His eyes linger on each of us in turn.

"I guess it wasn't that tough to figure out how to find me tonight."

"We got lucky," I say.

"Lucky's an interesting word for it," Mounce says, slips his jagged knife out from under his sweater.

"You can't do this," Dyl says.

"Why, 'cause underneath that punk rock anger you're just a bunch of whiny little maggots?"

"We're not really that angry," I say. "I mean, I personally am. About the ways our society is screwed up. Unfair. Rigged. But the punk rage is probably more of an aesthetic gesture, an exploration of—"

"Shut your hole!" Mounce says. "Goddamn, what a thing. What a Mongolian clusterfuck this turned out to be. Some A-rab contractor on Long Island gets all uppity about his fee and suddenly I'm bracing junkies and hairy commies on the Lower East Side. How the fuck does that happen? They say the apple never falls far from the tree, but you know what? I think your friend fell pretty fucking far from his daddy's date palm. That Massad is a tough bastard. I knew it wouldn't be worth it to bop him around. That's why I had to go to work on his kid."

"Where is Alan?" I say.

"I'd check potter's field."

"What?" I say.

"See this knife? I put this baby in his heart. Kid probably didn't feel a thing with all the dope in his system."

"No!" screams Hera. "No, it's not true!"

"Oh, man," Cutwolf whispers. "Oh, man . . ."

Mounce's words are like a haymaker I've been watching arc toward my face for days. My guts lurch, my legs wobble. I try to steady myself on the ice.

"You fools, on the other hand, are definitely going to feel something. But first, I've got to know. How did you nimrods get onto me at all?"

"Because," Dyl says, "you didn't have any papers."

"What, Poodlehead?"

"You've got to have the freaking papers."

"Oh, I do, do I?"

"You know something, Mounce," I say, the fear draining away even as my voice shakes with grief. "I think the fact that you're a psychopath might obscure the deeper truth that you are also a total moron. A smart killer wouldn't try to sell the bass of somebody he just whacked. What, you needed the money? It's just stupid. Sloppy. It's pretty sad, really. And maybe it didn't have to be this way. Maybe you didn't even have to be such a dud of a human being. In a smaller, more cohesive society, there would have been a place for you, a way for you to contribute, guarding the well or something. But not here. Here you just stumble around in your supreme nullity of thought and emotion, hurting people."

"Yeah," Dyl says. "You're just a big, dumb, abusive animal nobody could ever love!"

"Whoa, Nelly," Terry says.

Mounce's gaze swivels between Dyl and me. The decision about which of us to murder first must be excruciating, but he does arrive at a choice.

"Die, Poodle!" Mounce shouts. He digs into the ice with the toe of his blade and launches himself at Dyl, smashes him to the ground, sinks to a knee, raises his knife. Hera screams, pounds Mounce's back. Mounce turns and Dyl wraps himself around Mounce's knife arm in a scissor lock. I recall he'd been a high school wrestler, a bad one. Cutwolf and I charge over. Cutwolf tries to twist the knife out of Mounce's fist. I'm not sure how I think of it, but I pull the wig out of my jacket pocket, yank it over Mounce's face from behind, smother him.

"I have no shot," I hear one of the goons say.

"Nobody shoot!" Terry shouts.

Cutwolf howls, and from the corner of my eye I see blood spurt out of his hand, but he doesn't let go.

The four us, working in concert, somehow keep Mounce in check. He bellows into the wig.

"Frrrucck. Krilll deese frrruckers. . . ."

Sirens cut the night air. Car doors slam.

"Go!" somebody yells. "Go!"

I can hear people run, scramble, kick up gravel and snow. More shouts carry from the edge of the rink, but my world now is nothing but the ice under my knees, the wig in my fists, and the flesh mountain that writhes, heaves, beneath it.

"Police!" a voice calls behind me, from the direction of the gate. "Drop your weapon!"

The gunshots are loud, like being near a car when it backfires. My ears ring and an acrid stink fills the air. Still, I grip the wig with all my strength, my eyes squeezed shut, my hands and arms going numb. Mounce thrashes and I squeeze down again. The strain forces out a piss trickle that moistens my thermal underwear. More sirens wail and hands fall over me, snatch at my arms, peel them away.

"Jack," a voice says. "Let go!"

I know that voice.

"It's over, Jack. We have him. Let go."

I fall back on the ice, the wig still in my hand, stare into the upside-down face of Shad Fielden.

"Damn, Jack," he says. "You beast. Didn't think you had it in you."

TWENTY-THREE

It takes a while for my head to clear. Dozens of cops mill around the rink. Two of them kneel on Mounce, his hands cuffed behind his back. Others unlace his skates, hoist him up, march him in his socks across the ice.

Near the security booth paramedics crowd around a figure on the ground. I watch them untangle the cord to an oxygen mask. Fielden kneels beside me, clasps my elbow.

"That's the night watchman," he says.

"Leonard," I say.

"Poor bastard shouldn't have pulled down on us."

"He didn't have a gun."

"What are you trying to say?"

"Nothing. Just . . ."

"Take it easy," Fielden says. "You've just been through a violent and confusing experience."

Fielden's expression, on the other hand, says, *Leave it alone.*

"My friends . . ."

"Right over there."

Fielden points. Hera stands with Cutwolf. A paramedic wraps his hand. Dyl sits on a bench with Bollocks in his lap, strokes the dog's neck. Bollocks looks sad and sleepy but alive.

"You followed us from the Pinsk," I say. "Used us as bait."

"Don't be so paranoid," Fielden says, winks.

"Shad," a voice calls.

Detective Tabbert walks up, rubs his hands together, blows on them.

"What's up, Juan?"

"TV crew wants to interview you."

A man with a video camera on his shoulder stands with a woman gripping a bulky microphone.

"You do it," Fielden says.

"I did. They still want the pretty white boy."

"Such bullshit. Okay, I'm coming."

"Wait," I say. "Terry and those guys, did you get them?"

"What guys now?"

"The ones with the guns who shoved us into the rink. They work with Mounce."

"We didn't see any other guys. Just you twerps fighting Mounce on the ice. Actually, ask me, it was kind of funny to watch, like when they have André the Giant wrestle those midgets. Hey, tonight the midgets won."

"You've got to get those other men. Terry from the tower."

"Who? We saw some guys but couldn't ID them. Some other officers are looking into it."

"No, listen. If you followed us, you must have gotten a good look at them."

"No, you listen," Fielden says, his voice sharp now. "Don't tell me what I did or didn't see. I think you should go back downtown and be grateful we saved your sorry ass from that fucking Frankenstein. Before I bust you for trespassing and assault."

Fielden walks toward the news crew, wheels back.

"Shit, man, all this excitement, I didn't even tell you the good news."

"What's that?"

"Your buddy turned up. Alive."

We have to wait until the next afternoon to visit the Earl at Bellevue. Hera, Cutwolf, Dyl, and I head over.

We're all still shaken from the fight at the rink. Cutwolf's pick hand is a gauze hive.

I'm not sure what to expect, but the Earl looks pretty bad. Bandages cover his bruised, skinny chest. He breathes through tubes in his nose. His eyes are closed, crusted over, and his face seems stuck in a permanent wince. If you didn't know him as a glittering deity of underground legend, you might take him for some ordinary dude recently stabbed through the sternum.

Mr. Massad perches at his bedside, wipes his son's brow with a damp cloth, slips ice chips into his mouth.

"He's a little out of it now," he says. "Must be hurting. I told the nurses to go easy on the morphine. Might as well wean him while he heals. He was talking a lot before, but I think the drugs are wearing off a little."

Mr. Massad is cordial, but I can tell he's not thrilled to see us. We're maybe not the friends he'd wish for his son. Still, he compliments us on our efforts to find the Earl's would-be murderer, and Alan needs our good cheer. Mounce's knife just missed the Earl's heart, but it did do damage.

Now the Earl's eyes open.

"Your friends are here," Mr. Massad says.

A faint smile creeps over our front man's lips.

"Hey," I say.

"Jonathan," the Earl whispers.

"He's Jack now," Hera says.

"No, it's okay," I say. "Time enough for that."

"Jack," the Earl says. "Jack Shit."

"That's right," I say.

The Earl grins, closes his eyes.

We stay a few more minutes and Mr. Massad gives us the lowdown. The Earl managed to tell the police a bit of it, and they pieced together the rest. It seemed that Mounce found out Mr. Massad had a son in a band from one of Mr. Massad's foremen. Mounce used to be a bouncer, or a Mouncer, as he liked to describe his vocation back in the day, and still had some club contacts. These cronies told Mounce that a kid who fit the Earl's description used to hang out with Toad Molotov. When Mounce came around, Toad didn't want any trouble, told Mounce he could probably find the Earl at the Stop Pit, which he did. After telling the Earl how he'd found him, Mounce informed the Earl that he'd better convince his father to stop being such a hard-on about the invoice, or evil shit would ensue.

The Earl, of course, told him to fuck off. Then he said he'd pass the message along to his father for a hundred bucks. Mounce agreed, but didn't want to flash money in the bar. He led the Earl outside, said the cash was in his car and his car was parked at the end of Houston, near the FDR. The Earl knew better, but he was drunk and junk sick and he took a chance. Not his brightest moment. Next thing, they're across the highway in a park near the East River.

At this point, according to Mr. Massad's retelling of the Earl's report, Mounce made a speech about the old neighborhood and the importance of respecting one's elders and how maybe the problem was that people didn't listen to crooners like Dino anymore, which reminds me of a fact that both the Earl and I are aware of, namely that Nick Tosches, author of *Daryl Hall and John Oates: Dangerous Dances*, recently published a book about the aforementioned Rat Packer Dean Martin, but I doubt he remarked upon this to Mounce, and I'm afraid to ask Mr. Massad about it now. I'm the guy who wrote Mr. M. a castigating letter about his son and Baudelaire. Anyway, at this point, back in the park, the Earl got a little nervous, told Mounce that even just forty bucks would be fine, and that he'd also throw in the bass. "Sure," Mounce said, picked up the case from the grass, and started to walk away. "Hey," the Earl said, and here, Mr. Massad tells us, the Earl maybe regretted his decision to finish his thought. "What about my money?"

"Here's your fucking money," Mounce replied, and stuck his knife in the Earl's chest. Just as metal pierced bone, random shouts rose nearby. Some drunks near the river. At least that's how the Earl remembered it. He became less sure of the story after the knife went in, but Mr. Massad figures the shouts spooked Mounce, who pulled his blade out of the Earl and lumbered off.

"He must have gone back to Toad's the next night," I say now. "After trying to sell the bass at King Snake. He figured he'd killed the Earl—"

"My son's name is Alan," snaps Mr. Massad.

"Alan," I say. "Anyway, Mounce knew he had to cover his tracks."

"That's when we showed up," Cutwolf says.

"He must have had the bass with him," Hera says. "Was probably still taking it around town trying to sell it. And that stupid case of yours, with the broken latches."

"That's probably how your Rat fell out," Dyl says.

"We showed up just as Mounce was killing poor Toad," Cutwolf says. "We could have come a few minutes earlier and maybe things would be different. Spent too much time at that shitty Thorazine show."

"Hey," Hera says.

The Earl wheezes into speech.

"Toad is dead?"

I nod and the Earl's eyes go wide.

"When you get out," Cutwolf says, "we'll have some mint-jelly sandwiches and Cuervo in his honor."

Mr. Massad's head swivels.

"Or just the sandwiches," I say.

"How'd Alan get to the hospital anyway?" Hera asks.

"He walked," says a voice.

The Earl's mother stands in the doorway, Styrofoam coffee cups in either hand. I recognize her from the photograph, and the time she visited us.

"He was lying there in the park," she continues, "and he thought he was going to die. But he told me this. He said, 'Mama, I was lying there and it felt like I could just slip away but I remembered you and Dad and everybody, all we've been through, and I told myself I'm not dying like this. No way.' So, my little boy stood up with that terrible hole in him and he walked, my baby walked, all the blood pouring out of him, four blocks it must have been, before he passed out in front of a corner store. The owner called the ambulance. He was unconscious by then. Nobody knew who he was. No ID. Then, get this, when he does come to in the hospital, he gives a fake name, to protect his father. To protect his brothers and me. Can you imagine? That's Alan. What was that name he gave, dear?"

"Osterling, I think," Mr. Massad says. "Or, no, Osterberg."

"That's why it took so long to track him down," Mrs. Massad says. "That's what Detective Fielden said. He put it all together. He says we have enough now to really get this guy Mounce."

"It goes higher than Mounce," I say.

"You think I don't know that?" Mr. Massad says. "I'm the one who told you that."

"So what are we going to do?" I say.

"I'm going to take care of my boy. That's all that matters."

Now the nurse sticks her head in to tell us we have too many people in the room.

"Yes," Mr. Massad says. "Alan needs his rest."

We say quiet goodbyes to the Earl, and we're almost out the door when he calls to us. He props himself up awkwardly, painfully, it appears from his grimace, on his elbow.

"What about Artaud's?" he says.

"Obviously we'll cancel," Hera says.

"No," the Earl says. "Play the show. Do something. Instrumental, maybe. Sing a little if you want. We've got to stretch. It'll be a good exercise. Until I'm ready."

Cutwolf holds his bandaged hand up.

"Not even sure how much I can play."

"Dyl can back you up."

"Really?" I say.

"Really?" Dyl says.

"Yes," the Earl says.

"Holy shit," Dyl says, cradles himself in gentle ecstasy.

Mr. and Mrs. Massad look horrified that their son is even discussing this topic, but I feel a wild swell in my chest, the opposite of a killing blade.

No One Left to Come Looking for You

The Shits live!
"Are you sure?" Cutwolf says.
"Play the fucking show."
"Okay, then," I say.
The Earl slumps back into his pillow.

TWENTY-FOUR

Saturday afternoon we load into Artaud's. The Garage started as an artists' squat in the '80s, and it's still a collective, with anarchist sculpture exhibits and music shows on the weekends. The stage is just a filthy riser of unfinished pinewood and the bar is a board laid over two sawhorses, but they've got decent sound and lots of off-brand booze. Toad once told me that the name Artaud's has nothing to do with the famous director of the Theatre of Cruelty, but that the space, a large cement bay with high windows and oil stains on the floor, used to be a repair garage run by a French Canadian mechanic, though he might have been fucking with me.

Crystal the booker meets us at the door. She's still got her sparkly crash helmet.

"Dogcut," she says.

"Cutwolf," Cutwolf says.

"Oh, sorry."

"You work here?" I say.

"Just started, yeah."

"How's the brain damage?" Cutwolf asks.

"Good days and dab days."

"How about today?"

"TBA."

Crystal watches us haul our gear from Dyl's van.

"You can't park here," she says. "Load in and then move the van somewhere down the street."

"Will do," Dyl says.

Dyl is not just our driver and roadie now. Per the Earl's orders, tonight he's a Shit. Soon he will unfurl his vaunted sonic curtain. We've reworked a few of our songs into extended improvisations within a rigorous chordal framework. Just don't call them jams.

If we get a clean recording off the board, maybe we can release tonight's performance as an EP, something for the Shits diehards, swan song or not.

Crystal tells us to hurry up and sound check, because while we might consider this our big evening, we're here to open for two other bands, the Bed Fellows and Count Fistula, and they are scheduled to load in soon. Also, and this really burns my ass, we just found out that Mongoose Civique is headlining a Geffen showcase at CB's tonight. It's not really direct competition because they probably won't go on until long after we're done, and we don't exactly draw the same crowd. Our fans tend not to be tasteless sycophants, posturing dullards, and industry trash, but are instead brave pioneers of the human spirit.

Slightly different type.

I join the others onstage, strap on my Hondo, plug in.

The kid at the board asks us to each play a few bars alone, and after that we roll into "Spores," a Shits warhorse. Dyl wasn't kidding about his curtain. He hunches over the Les Paul goldtop he's plundered from the King Snake wall, and the textures he summons shimmer with thick majesty. Cutwolf, his hand wrapped tight, plays jagged loops over Dyl's sustain as Hera hammers away. I supply the subatomic throb playing my Hondo through a new Rat pedal Dyl scored me from the store.

It's scary. We have heft, we have craft. We come to the end of the song, stare at each other, giddy.

"That was pretty damn good," the kid says.

I never imagined we could sound strong without the Earl. Maybe tonight's show will reveal another side of the Shits. Like the Earl said, we have to stretch.

"What about vocals?" the kid asks.

We gaze over at the microphone in its stand, lonely as Elijah's cup.

"We won't be doing much," I say. "Maybe lean in for the occasional shout."

"I'll keep it hot."

"Thanks," I say.

The Garage is not officially open, but we head to the bar for the first of our two complimentary beverages. It's always a drag, how stingy these clubs get with the drink tickets. We'll have a few whiskeys or beers before the show, and once we've played we have to wait hours for the other bands to finish before we can load out. There's nothing to do but swill alcohol. If we're lucky, the booker will take pity and slip us more tickets, or the bartender will be a weirdo and thus a natural Shits ally, or else some actual fan with cash flow will stand us more rounds. Most nights, though, our bar tab puts a gruesome dent in our door cut. It almost makes me want to join a straight edge band.

Tonight's bartender is a stranger and he takes my ticket with a cold professionalism that hints at a dearth of future freebies. Oh well. He pushes my whiskey over and I take a sip, feel a hand on my ass. It squeezes.

"Hey, sweet cheeks," a voice behind me says.

"Corrina."

She slides up beside me in a plaid jacket and longshoreman's wool cap, gives me a big hug. I haven't seen her since the night of the opening, but I feel a warm jolt in her arms right now, like what I pictured a lover's embrace could be, but never was, not even with Vesna. I wonder if my mother and father ever experienced such a surge with each other. They must have, back in the early years, before me, before Andy Warhol, before Bink.

"How was sound check?" she says.

"Really good. I don't know why we didn't ask Dyl to play with us before."

"You said it was because he was lame and used words like 'chops' and 'axe.'"

"I know," I say, look down at my drink. "Maybe I was too tough on him."

"You sound like a dad."

"Oh yeah?"

"I'd like to meet your parents," Corrina says.

"You sure about that?"

"Yeah."

"I thought you were going to call me this week. After you and Mateo talked."

"I wanted to last night. It got late."

"Were you with him?"

"Yes."

"Did you—"

"Look, Jack. Me and Mateo are over. We really loved each other for a while. Or thought we did. But the marriage? That was more of a green card thing. It's tricky. Can you be patient?"

"Can you hide his boots when I come over?"

"I could probably do that for you," Corrina says, and we

kiss again, hoover up each other's tongue. I'm almost ready to suggest we leave when I remember we have a show to play, not a thing I'd normally forget.

Now Hera and Cutwolf rush over. Cutwolf waves a copy of the *Daily News* in my face.

"Just found this in the can. What the fuck?"

I snatch the newspaper, study the headline: "SUSPECT IN DOWNTOWN MURDER HANGS HIMSELF IN JAIL CELL." Next to the article is a photograph of Heidy Mounce.

"There's no fucking way," Cutwolf says. "There's no way he did that to himself."

"Cut," I say. "Calm down. We don't know. People do that. He was looking at serious time."

"I don't buy it."

I'm not sure I do either, but for some reason it feels really important to believe the police official quoted in the article, to trust the *Daily News* reporters, to conclude that though there are deep seams of misery and darkness in this city, it's not all by design, that there are still some people on the up-and-up. Maybe I just don't want anything to further disrupt my tongue-jousting session with Corrina.

"Doesn't make sense," Dyl says. "Guys like Mounce thrive in prison. Probably not his first choice of residence, but not worth offing yourself over."

"Right, Dyl," I say. "Because you have such expert insight into the psychology of brutal criminals."

"Whatever, Jack," Cutwolf says. "I bet you think Oswald acted alone too."

"No, dude," I say. "Obviously Brian Jones was on the knoll. Can we just focus on the show?"

"Jack's right," Hera says. "We were in the goddamn bitching chair during sound check. Let's stay on the rock donkey. Dyl, you were a right beautiful cunt up there."

It's a treat to hear Hera talk in her bizarre, familiar way, our private band lingo mixed in with her awkward Brit approximations. We all relax a bit.

"Thanks," Dyl says.

"Hey," Crystal calls from the door. "Which one of you is Jack Shit? Guy here says he has something for you. Shad something?"

"Let him in," I say.

Fielden moves out of the square blast of door light into the cool dark of the garage. Today it's a white parka with a furry collar, mirrored shades. Alpine Serpico. He lays a long hardshell guitar case on the plywood bar.

"Found this at Mounce's apartment after we busted him," he says.

"Looks oddly familiar," I say.

"Oh, drat," Fielden says, winks at me. "I neglected to log it."

Both latches hang off the case, the whole thing wrapped with a bungee cord.

"Thank you," I say, untie the cord, lift out my beloved Fender Jazz Bass, run my hand over the frets and pickboard, check for chips and cracks.

"Copacetic?" Fielden says.

"Yes," I say. "It looks fine."

"Good. Now I hope, truly, that all of our business is concluded."

"We heard about Mounce," Cutwolf says.

"Yeah," Fielden says. "Happens."

"What happens?" Hera says.

Fielden seems about to say something, sighs.

"Have a great show," he says, finally. "I'd stay, but I don't think it's my cup of tea. I'm more of a speed metal guy."

"I thought you weren't into music," I say.

"Who told you that?"

"You did."

"Don't worry," Hera says. "Detective Fielden fibs about a lot of things."

"Excuse me?"

"I talked to my sister."

"Your sister?"

"Calliope?"

"Right. Her."

"She said something pretty interesting about you."

"I told her about the chlamydia as soon as I knew."

"Not that."

"Oh."

"She said that you're not from Brooklyn at all. That you're a faculty brat. Your dad was chairman of the English department. You grew up in a big house next to campus."

"Okay, so what?"

"She said Fredric Jameson is your godfather."

"Not like officially or anything."

"All your talk about us. You're a tourist too."

"Maybe, but at least I'm getting paid for it."

"We're getting thirteen percent of the door," Cutwolf says.

"You know," Fielden says, "for a while I figured I was the only guy on the force who'd read Foucault. But get this: it's a lot more than you think. Anyway, that's the past. Let's deal with the situation at hand, shall we? Hey, I've got a solution. How about you mind your own business and stop sticking your beaks in shit you will never understand. And we can all return to our regularly scheduled programming. You live your wannabe lives, I go back to putting assholes away. Capiche?"

"You going to put yourself away?" Cutwolf says.

"The fuck you say," Fielden says.

We all just stand there, peer around for eyewitnesses to whatever's coming next. Both Crystal and the bartender have slipped off. Only the sound kid remains. He's in a headphones world, eyes closed as he bobs to a mystery beat.

Before anything else happens, some men crowd the doorway, shout and jostle. It's the Bed Fellows. They drag an amp and a kick drum over the threshold.

"You guys seen Crystal?"

Fielden ducks out behind them.

After a few seconds, I rush after him.

"Jack!" Cutwolf says, but I'm running.

"Hey!" I call to Fielden at the corner.

He whirls around in his shades.

"What is it, man?"

"I'm going to figure it out," I say. "The whole thing."

"There's nothing to figure out, Jack. You know who the bad guys are. The rest of it is just people covering their asses."

"Oh, so you're admitting to a cover-up?"

Crystal and the bartender lean against the garage wall, smoke, watch us.

"Come here, buddy!" Fielden shouts. "I'm sorry, man. Give me a hug!"

Fielden gathers me into an embrace, hustles me down a narrow alley behind Artaud's, pushes me against a dumpster. He opens his coat to flash his Glock.

"It's always such a nightmare when a white kid gets doinked

down here. So much fucking brouhaha. And paperwork. But it always fades eventually."

"Are you threatening me?"

"I'm sharing."

"Didn't seem to be much brouhaha about Toad."

"He was a different animal. A reptile."

"Toads are amphibians," I say.

"Keep pushing, pal," Fielden says, puts his hand on the grip of his pistol.

I wonder if Fielden really means to shoot me, if I've finally arrived at the end of everything, by which I mean the end of Jack Shit, one of this world's countless unfortunate travelers, and by definition the end of Jonathan Liptak, too, who came to this mighty city to live, to love, to nourish his brethren with cascades of noise, to revel in sweat-ecstasies of sonic communion.

Now I might become just another dead guy, dead like sweet Grandpa Abe, or the garbagehead in the garbage can, or the old man with the Warren Beatty rental I found lying in his driveway, that last-breath gossamer death bubble on his lips.

I'm going to be dead like Toad.

I wish I had more time, but even so, a strange, calm wave, like some polite tsunami of foam-crested cosmic wisdom, breaks over me. I recall the motto of my kindergarten teacher: "You get what you get, and you don't get upset." What else, in the end, is there to say? This is what I get. And while a part of me is very fucking upset, another part prepares, if that's even possible, for Fielden to pull out his plastic gun and send a slug through my skull.

But I never find out if that fate awaits, because a low growl rises from the behind the dumpster. We both peer over to see a figure crawl out from the narrow crevice between the dumpster and the alley's brick wall. This creature is some kind of diseased bird with jaundiced eyes and a breast of dirty synthetic mesh under greasy denim wings.

"Fuck," the creature says, stands. "Trying to get some sleep around here."

"Jesus," Fielden says. "Goddamn skell."

"Don't like that word," the Denim Ghoul says.

"I don't care. Get the fuck out of here, skell."

"You get out of here. You're in my home. One of my homes."

"I don't think you understand," Fielden says, lifts his badge on its chain out from under his shirt.

"Oh, believe me, I understand," the Ghoul says. "Same-o same-o with you motherfuckers. Always rousting us, pushing us around. I'm fucking tired of it. So why don't you leave this kid alone and go back to your pigpen."

Fielden's face goes tight and he looks about to pounce when a voice comes from the mouth of the alley.

"Francis!"

Detective Tabbert stands about twenty feet away.

"Oh, hey, Juan," the Ghoul says, leans back on the dumpster.

"I thought you wanted to wait in the car," Fielden says to his partner.

"I did. But you took so long. Listen, fellas, Detective Fielden apologizes for his manner. He's still learning community relations. Let's go, Shad."

"You know this bum?"

"Francis? Sure. I used to walk a beat down here. We go way back. Right, Francis?"

Francis nods.

"Well, I've got him on obstruction and interfering with the work of an active—"

191

"You know what, Detective," Tabbert says. "That's enough for today."

Tabbert jerks his thumb over his shoulder. Fielden stares at the Ghoul, at me, spits on the ground, stalks off. Tabbert walks over to the dumpster.

"He almost killed me," I say.

"Don't be dramatic," Tabbert says.

"Seriously," the Denim Ghoul says.

"He won't bother you anymore," Tabbert says. "You have my word."

"What good is that?"

Tabbert goes very still, lets his sharp, shining eyes swim into mine.

"Okay," I say.

"Look, son, things are complicated, but I have control of the situation. And I hear the kid is recovering. And the security guard, well, they say he'll walk again. So maybe we can just put a cork in this thing."

"A cork?" I say. "And that's it? Three hundred pounds of satanic insanity hangs himself in his jail cell with no note. My friend gets a knife in the chest. You guys gun down an unarmed night watchman at an ice rink. And a dude whose only crime was sometimes being an overbearing douche and not quite working past his rage about the Reagan revolution is murdered in his apartment. And it's all just swept under the rug? With a cork, or whatever? Why? Just to protect the rich, crooked fucks who run this city?"

"Also to serve," the Ghoul chirps. "To protect and *serve* the crooked fucks."

"Take a walk, Francis," Tabbert says.

The Denim Ghoul shrugs, ambles off.

Tabbert buttons his overcoat, smooths his tie. Today it's shotgun-toting Elmer Fudds on yellow silk. He smiles, gazes at me.

"Rock steady, Monsieur Merde," he says, turns back down the alley.

TWENTY-FIVE

"**H**ey, y'all," Crystal shouts through the soundboard microphone. "You ready for the shitshow! Give it up for the Shits!"

We climb up to the stage to some scattered hoots, stare out at a crowd of about three dozen. Some must be Artaud's regulars, but a few I recognize from previous gigs. Our loyal legion. Some special guests have also materialized. Trancine and Corrina chat together near the bar. Vincent, with his impeccable Mohawk, leans against a concrete pillar. He raises his pint glass in salute, turns to talk to Gary, my one-thumbed predecessor in the Annihilation of the Soft Left.

I'm touched they're all here, but the next familiar face I see makes my gut clench. Toward the back, clutching a can of beer, stands my Green Thumb nemesis, Tony the Turd, a lurid smirk on his beaver mug. I vow in this moment not to let his corpse-stench soul undo me. If this enemy of feeling wants to stand in the vicinity of our truth, so be it. It's just too bad the Earl won't be here to show the Turd what a true artist can do with a microphone, the darkness, and a human heart. Maybe Tony could be saved, Rapunzel'd out of his tower of priggish self-regard. Or maybe not.

Here's another odd thing: without even thinking about it, I've strapped on my Hondo. The Fender looked fine, but after everything that's happened, the instrument has somehow lost its magic. Too much bad mojo. Maybe I'll even sell it. Crazy, I know, given what I've been through to get it back, but maybe that's life. By the time you find what you've been seeking, you're a different seeker.

We may lack a front man tonight, but we have not forgotten the stage rules we set down long ago: No casual banter with each other or the audience. No pandering or self-deprecation or attempts to appear down-to-earth. Never break character (though your character may mutate as you go), never break ranks. Honor the menace. Honor the mayhem. Honor the clown gods of honest witness. Honor raw feeling, peeled feeling. No winking.

One night at the Vortex, Hera violated protocol, waved to her sister in the audience, shouted, "Hey, sis!"

We kicked her out of the Shits for two days.

But now it seems that for all those nights Dyl watched us play and learned our songs, he still doesn't savvy the code. I watch him jaw with some guy in a flannel shirt at the edge of the stage. The dude even leans his arms up on our monitor, like we're all pals at the hootenanny. Cutwolf lifts up his wolf mask, shoots me a look. I adjust my wig, walk over there.

"Oh, hey, Jack," Dyl says. "This is my friend—"

"Friend time is over," I say.

"Talk to you later," Dyl says.

"And get your fucking arms off the monitor," I say.

"Sure, man," the guy says, sneers.

"I think you should leave," I say.

"Jack, come on," Dyl says.

"No," I say. "He needs to go."

"Way to cultivate a following, asshole," the guy says.

"You don't deserve to follow us," I say. "Or even hear us. Why don't you head over to CB's? Mongoose Civique will be on later."

"Maybe I will. Hear some real music."

"If by 'real' you mean the soundtrack to the shadow farce in Plato's Cave, be my guest."

"What the fuck?"

"Scram, pal."

"Cool friends you got," the guy says to Dyl, shakes his head, slinks off.

"What was that for?" Dyl says.

"For the sanctity of our endeavor," I say.

"You must really hate the audience."

"No," Cutwolf says, leans in, his mint-green guitar low on his hips. "It's the exact opposite, Dyl. I can't believe you don't get that. And now look at us. We're up here talking to each other like a bunch of chumps."

Hera rises from her drum stool, joins our confab.

"Play already!" some lout calls.

"What's the holdup?" Hera says.

"All right," I say. "Let's do 'Ghost Strap.'"

"That's too fraught for me," Hera says.

"Or 'Shipwreck.' Or 'Rosenberg.'"

"Fuck, this is fucked," Cutwolf says.

"Hey, Shits!" somebody yells. "Shit or get off the pot!"

"Maybe we should get off the stage and then come back on," Dyl says.

"That's worse," Hera says.

"It's all ruined," Cutwolf says.

It's true. We're stranded up on the stage in an anxious cluster like the middle-school jazz band before the big Christmas concert. No mystery. No madness. No derangement of the societal spectacle. It's a sad start to what I secretly hoped would be the show that kept the Shits together.

"Yip yip!" I bark.

"What?" says Dyl.

"Yip yip!"

Cutwolf nods, grins, strides back into position. Hera slips back behind her drums.

"Wait, what are we doing?" Dyl whispers.

"Watch and learn," I say.

Now I lean into the microphone.

"Good evening. We're the Shits. We've come to teach you a new way to be free. It's an arduous journey. Some of you won't make it. And when that happens, we'll forget all about you. Because that's the way of our cruel world. Ask Toad Molotov. This song is called 'Orbit City Comedown.' It's about how truly alone all of you are and how much you lie to yourselves about it so you don't blow your brains out but maybe you should. Onetwothreefour!"

We rip into the song hard, and for about eight seconds it's pretty tight, but everything falls apart fast. My bass work is too jittery, never quite locks in with Hera's beat. Dyl's sonic curtain is more like a tattered camisole. Cutwolf looks around bewildered, a few strings popped. It's all a tinny, off-key clatter. We haven't sounded this bad, this anemic, in years. Hot shame presses my chest and the insides of my eyes, but we grind on until the end of the song, finish a merciful minute early.

It's hard to make out the room under the stage lights, but it's easy to hear the embarrassed silence. I hear people shuffle off toward the bar or the door. There are mutters, titters. I'm pretty sure I hear the Turd's unmistakable guffaw. Dyl paces the stage with a hurt-puppy look. Maybe he thinks it's all his fault. I turn to face my bass cabinet, fiddle with some dials, hide. Hera crouches behind her kit.

I guess with Dyl in our ranks we can rock a sound check, but we can't bitch out when it counts.

The Shits are nothing without the Earl, and this show is doomed.

But now I hear an odd slapping sound, almost like applause. I peer over my shoulder at the audience, or whatever is left of it, see two pale arms in motion.

"Oh, yes!" comes a voice, stark and shredded, but with honey in the hollows. "All right!"

It's the Banished Earl, in something like the flesh. He claps and shouts and leaps to the stage. His hospital gown flutters out from his naked ass. His skin is almost purple under the lights. His eyes are pinned and I notice he's got a few glassine envelopes of heroin in his cupped hand. The Earl sees me notice, grins, pinches one bag open, and snorts it up. He steps up to each of us in turn and does not speak, looks deep into our eyes until satisfied. The room is still quiet but now everyone is back, pressed in around us. The Earl is magnetic even in his ruined state. Maybe more so. The role he plays tonight is Dead Man. He slips off his johnny, tosses it to the crowd. The wound in his chest is pus-rimed, crusted. It bristles with hideous stitch-work. The Earl skips across the stage like a nimble nymphet in a garden, blows kisses to the audience, reaches down, and gently strokes the cheek of a bruiser with a shaved head. The brute lifts his face to the Earl with a wonder-smacked grin.

The Earl steps up to the microphone.

"Hello, brothers and sisters. I've returned from the grave to serenade you sad fucks tonight."

"We love you!" somebody shouts from the darkness.

"And I love all of you. Truly. We are the Shits, and we come to bleed for you. See?"

The Earl tugs at his stitches. The crowd howls as he rips at the top suture, works his way down the wound. Blood ribbons thinly on his chest. It's the color of molasses in the rack lights.

"I am the world's finest striptease artist," the Earl whispers.

"Take it off!" somebody says, whistles.

"I'm gonna step right outta my skin!" the Earl screams.

The crowd roars, and Hera starts a count-off with her sticks, and the way she does it makes it clear to us, even to Dyl, that we are about to launch into the most ferocious version of "Bag Fever (Ain't Gonna Break)" we've ever attempted, and in a moment we are in the magic citadel of our sound, the walls draped with Dyl's curtains, restored to their original weave and grandeur, and then we are not in any kind of citadel or castle at all but in a body, or, rather, we are a body, have become one, a giant body that lunges up at the sky, and the Earl is the immense and beautiful head, Hera the arms and the legs as she strokes, churns, kicks up toward the stratosphere, and Cutwolf and Dyl are the guts and I'm the heartbeat, as always, the underpulse of this complex vibrating machine-animal, and now we soar, we drive, we whirl. We play as we've never played before, and probably ever will again. The crowd, estranged now for eternity from all that is petty and known, match our noise with their own surges of happy frenzy, and we drive on and up and through. The Earl leads us. The Earl shouts, jerks, twirls, squirms, a jester, a dervish, or the adept of some sacred diamond-sharp agony, while symphonies of sensation explode across his face, and he continues to tear his chest open, like a romance-novel lover eager to escape his blouse. Blood slides down his skinny belly, into the gullies of his hips and thighs, his black nest of pubic hair. His voice, in perfect pitch, in a high gospel wail, surfs our barrel wave of amplified knurl and crunch.

> *God, Allah, Yaweh,*
> *You mean motherfucker*
> *You underachiever*
> *You gotta deliver*
> *Your sorrow-struck boy*
> *From bag fever*
> *(Ain't gonna break!)*
> *Bag fever*
> *(Ain't gonna break!)*

Just before the last chorus the Earl's body collapses, folds down on itself in fast spasms. Tough to tell whether it's stage antics, an OD, fatal blood loss, or all of the above, and I look over to Cutwolf, who offers up a wince and a shrug. It's too late to turn back. We finish the song, even play the new experimental outro we concocted for an Earl-less performance.

The crowd screams, chants our name: "Shits! Shits! Shits!"

Tony the Turd pushes up to the stage, gazes up at me in stunned worship. I hock an almond-shaped gob of dark phlegm into his face, but I do it in character, the character of his newly acknowledged superior, and from love.

The Turd bows.

The Earl stays motionless.

But after a moment his shoulders buck and he rises to his elbows. A column of vomit rockets out of his mouth. He rolls onto his back. His wound, the loosened flaps of stitch-burst meat, are black with floor grime, his torso smeared with blood.

The Earl reaches out and gropes for the microphone, pushes it to his lips for some lazy fellatio.

"Okay, then," he rasps. "Perhaps you've earned the right to hear another of our delectable compositions. But don't get cocky."

He flicks a finger at his penis, his shrunken mushroom.

"Ha, cocky."

A thin rope of urine spurts out of the tip, glints in the lights.

The Earl rolls over, lifts himself to his knees. I squat down beside him.

"We can stop," I say.

"Never," the Earl whispers. "But thank you."

"For what?"

"For your valor. For your friendship. Your loyalty."

"I'm leal," I say, look for signs of my hero in those beautiful, gone black eyes.

"This next one is dedicated to all the murdered ones!" the Earl shouts into the microphone. "The martyrs of Alphabet City. Their deaths will be avenged! By rock 'n' roll! And the children. Let's not forget the children. . . ."

The Earl tries to stand, pitches over again, sprawls out on the splintered planks. This time he stays still. But I'm pretty certain he's breathing.

We hurl ourselves into "Spores" once more.

It's even better than sound check.

TWENTY-SIX

It's almost spring, and I'm Jonathan again.

It's almost spring, and it's winter more than ever.

I've been hunkered down in the Rock Rook without phone service for the better part of two days. They call it the Storm of the Century, what swept up from the Gulf of Mexico and dumped high heaps of snow across the Eastern Seaboard. The radio says hundreds are dead. Many are missing, millions trapped in their homes, their driveways.

It's been a quiet, lonely time in the Rock Rook in general. The storm just made the world whiter, deader.

I live alone here now. The Banished Earl has repaired to a rehab upstate. He mailed me a postcard a few weeks ago:

> I have decided to live. The Shits will live too. Sending new lyrics soon. Don't worry, I haven't lost my edge. It now glitters in the hard sunlight of becoming.

These were glad tidings.

The Earl did manage to rise up again that night at Artaud's, and we blasted through another song or two. By then his father and brothers had arrived. They wrestled his naked, bleeding body off the stage and stuffed him into an American Builders minivan. It's hard to imagine a more legendary close to a show.

It's also hard, despite the Earl's postcard, to picture the future of the Shits. Cutwolf has fled New York for Cincinnati, his home city. He says he's looking into grad school, maybe library science, which surprises me. I've never seen him go into a library except to take a crap.

An even bigger shock is that Cutwolf took Crystal with him. She said the East Coast was giving her brain-damaged brain a headache. They've rented a house near the university. Sometimes they sleep together, but Crystal told Cut she likes him mostly as roommate.

Trancine had dumped him not long after our last show, said he could keep the wolf mask as a memento.

"What about you and Hera?" I asked him a few days before he left.

"What about her?"

"I've always felt like there was something between you two."

"Don't be silly," Cutwolf said, but with a strain in his voice that made me wonder how long he could stand to deny it.

As for Hera, she is back with Wallach. Or at least she's back in Thorazine. They played another show on Bethune Street a few weeks ago. They have a new member, a woman on theremin.

Dyl and I went to the show and when we heard that song again we both realized that what Wallach was saying was "scapegoat." Dyl seemed disappointed, and skeptical about his initial mistake.

"Hera must have made Wallach change it," he said. "And you can't sand down a goat."

"We'll never know," I said.

Speaking of Dyl, he and I have been messing around with some new riffs. It could even come to something. I hope we can lure Hera back, or maybe find a new drummer. We might buy an ad in the classifieds. The other day I saw a listing for a guitarist another band put in the *Village Voice*. One of the influences they cited was the Shits. I trembled when I saw us named. Maybe it hasn't all been for nothing. Maybe we've left something behind.

Most of my loneliness is on account of Corrina. Things were really good for a while. She even moved into the Rock Rook for a few weeks. We cleaned it up, carried in some decent furniture from the curb, made the Earl's sarcophagus our master bedroom. I figured it was a fine plan until I knew whether the Earl was coming back. Corrina and I cooked spaghetti, drank coffee and wine, read each other passages from the sidewalk canon, which Corrina expanded to include some women, like her beloved Hildegard. We played records and fucked on fresh sheets I bought at the ninety-nine-cent store.

It felt like love, at least from my end.

But after a while, Corrina seemed to grow restless. Her friend Monica's success in the art world made Corrina resent our tiny abode, our hand-to-mouth life. Mateo went back to Madrid for a while and Corrina moved back into their old apartment. She says it's just temporary, so she can get some work done, but we don't see each other that much and I'm worried she's begun to drift away.

The other day I got an invitation to the opening of her film installation, *Trinity's Company: Bingen/Tripper.* She must have put my name on the list, but she hasn't mentioned it to me. It's hard to fathom whether she wants me to attend, but either way I'm pleased to know that in some obscure gallery's tight alcove, on a monitor behind a black curtain, all comers can watch me on a daylong loop fall to my knees and bug my eyes through a veil of woman blood.

Maybe it's my way of being with Corrina a little more frequently, even as I fester here alone.

Thing is, based on my current supply of rice, booze, and canned beans, I could go weeks without leaving the Rock Rook. I even have a little bag of shake I've been smoking through a half-rotten apple pipe. But today I discovered my tragic miscalculation: I failed to lay in extra cans of coffee. I just drank my last cup, and I'm not ready to kick caffeine.

I've already commenced my methodical layering process, beginning with the thermals, when the phone rings.

My line's been out for two days, and I checked it an hour ago, but now I hear breathing on the other end. It's odd to say somebody's breathing sounds familiar, but it does.

"Cut?"

"Jack?"

"Jonathan," I say.

"Oh."

"Maybe I was really Jonathan all along."

"Okay."

"What's up?" I say.

"Nothing, man. Just, you know, checking in. You doing all right?"

"You mean the blizzard?"

"The blizzard? Oh, yeah. Of course. You guys get buried?"

"Definitely."

"Crazy."

"Yeah."

"Yeah, we got a little."

"Yeah."

Conversation was never exactly free-flowing with old Craig Dunn, but the stiffness grates more now.

"So, what's up, man?" I say, a little sharp.

"I don't know. I got a postcard from the Earl."

"Me too."

"Figured," Cutwolf says. "How'd he sound in yours?"

"Good. Said he was writing new lyrics."

"Nice."

"What about yours?"

"Well, he sounded amped. Happy."

"Good."

"He asked if I had a car in Cincinnati. Wanted me to drive to Delaware, where the rehab is. Said he was ready to leave."

"No," I say. "He's supposed to be there for six months at least."

"I know."

"Don't go."

"I'm not. Believe me. But it makes me worry. What's he thinking?"

"Well, we know what he's thinking. Damn, I hope he's okay."

Cutwolf doesn't answer for a moment.

"Me too, man," he says. "Me too."

"But I can't . . ."

"What?"

"I wouldn't be able to go looking for him," I say. "If he . . . I couldn't do it again."

"I hear you."

"Let's just hope he stays. Gets his shit together."

"I wonder what he's like with his shit together," Cutwolf says.

It's a good point. We hang in silence for a moment.

"Okay, man," I say. "I've got to go. I'm out of coffee."

"Wait. Jonathan?"

"What?"

"I'm sorry."

"For what?" I say.

"For leaving. For leaving you. But I had to go. Do you understand? Everything was so nuts."

"We got close," I say.

"Close to what?"

"The portal."

"The portal?"

"Yeah."

"I guess we did," Cutwolf says. "Hey, Jonathan?"

"What?"

"Don't quit."

"Whatever," I say, hang up. I sit there on a milk crate, one leg in my thermals, stare at the wall.

It's late afternoon when I finally push my way outside, climb the snow mound that blocks the front of my building, head off into the soft white void. The sun is a low smear in the gray sky. I sink to my knees in frozen drifts, carve a narrow canal down the street.

They've boarded up the speed bodega. The food bodega is a few blocks away. I pass the Pinsk and the Stop Pit. Everything is locked, gated, skirted in snow.

I think I'm all alone out here when I hear a crunch, a whoosh, some grunts. I turn to watch a man on skinny skis pole past me. Far off, another figure slaps along on snowshoes. Who are these closet frontiersmen who wait for certain weather to reveal themselves? Are they trapping furs in Tompkins Square Park?

I trudge toward the food bodega. They've dug out a little trench at the entrance. I stamp my feet, slip inside.

It's warm in here and I linger near the door, until the guy at the register scowls.

"Café Bustelo?" I say.

The man points to an aisle, where I find a sublime array of yellow cans. I grab two, plus a quart of milk, carry it all to the counter.

"Hell of a storm," I say.

"Superstorm," the man says.

"Storm of the Century," I say.

The man says nothing, watches me, wary, not unkind.

"Sorry," I say, because I'm weeping. I squeeze my eyes to stanch the tears, wipe my face on my sleeve. I remember when Corrina chided me for crying too much on the way to the gallery. Maybe with a few months gone by, I've earned a new allotment of jags.

The man nods, as though to convey to me his considered opinion that I am now ready to leave his bodega.

The cold air stings my eyes and I look for my old trail. I want to follow my boot prints home, like I'm my own King Wenceslas, but after only a few steps I accidentally veer off, march new holes in the snow.

About a block from the Rock Rook, I nearly trip over some trash. When my sopped sneaker hooks a plastic yard bag, I hear a moan.

Under a blanket of snow and garbage, a man sits up against a mailbox. His skin is nearly blue, but I recognize his mesh shirt and ice-encrusted jean jacket.

"Francis?"

The Denim Ghoul moans again.

"Francis, are you okay?"

The Ghoul's eyes swivel up.

"Do you remember me?" I say.

The Denim Ghoul studies my face.

"Yes," he says, lifts a stiff hand, digs into his pocket. "Do you want to buy some batteries?"

"Yeah, I'll buy them. But wait. Do you want to come home with me?"

The Ghoul shrinks a little, eyes me.

"What do you mean? I'm not really in any condition to—"

"No, just . . . you want to thaw out?" I say. "I've got coffee and beans. And whiskey. We can listen to records. Talk about the new president."

"He's from Arkansas."

"I know that."

"But not Arkansas now. Arkansas a thousand years in the future. They've sent a robot king."

"Makes sense," I say. "Anyway, you want to come over?"

"That would be swell."

"Okay, then."

"Only one problem. I can't feel my legs. I don't think I can stand up."

It takes me a moment to collect his things, his shredded shopping bags and torn duffel. I sling the duffel over my shoulder, slide the bags on my wrists with my own from the bodega. I squat, scoop him up. He's frighteningly light.

"Giddyup," the Ghoul commands, throws an arm around my neck.

"I'm giddying," I say.

The way is slow, slick with ice, and by the time we reach my door, the sun has long set. A few stars wink hazy in the

209

deepening twilight. The universe, I suppose, has a million, billion, trillion stars. In the night sky of New York City, you're lucky to see two or three. Still, maybe it's enough to know the rest are out there somewhere, twinkling for somebody, burning down to dust.